Heart Stones & DIAMONDS

Linda Boulanger

Heart Stones & Diamonds
A Wings & Whispers Love Story
©2019 by Linda Boulanger

Edited by Grace Augustine/Edits with a Touch of Grace
Initial Cover Design by Vicki Eaton – All Cover Book Design (cover changes made by Tell~Tale Book Covers, by permission)
Interior Design by Tell~Tale Book Covers
First released as part of the *Between the Tides* Anthology

Published by TreasureLine Publishing

Also available in eBook publication

PRINTED IN THE UNITED STATES OF AMERICA

I dedicate this book to Kristen Hansell
whose heart stone gift from Alaska
inspired the idea for this story.
It may not be shiny or colorful,
but it's my favorite – a true treasure.

And to all who have known love,
lost love, and have yet to find it…
Trust your heart.

Chapter 1

Kalen pressed hard against the water, driving his massive form deeper. His body sliced through the depths as he picked up speed, rolling, darting in and out of the pillars of an abandoned cathedral before he arched up and over a reef of sparkling coral. He spun around, glancing side to side, looking at the entourage he'd picked up along the way. All the creatures of the sea relished a swim with the mighty water dragon shifter, each doing his or her best to keep up with the Blue Bullet.

He huffed, blowing bubbles several feet in front of him that sent some of the smaller fish spiraling as he slowed his pace, thinking of his nickname. Kalen wasn't particularly fond of it. He'd have much preferred something more aquatic sounding, more royal. Especially considering who he was.

He blinked his big blue eyes, feeling his importance in every fiber of his enormous body... until he heard one of the seals again barking the nickname that he'd been given by the younger creatures of the sea.

He rolled his eyes, along with his body. The motion caused a ripple that tossed about a couple of young turtles, a dolphin, and one of the young seals. They all squealed in delight, making him laugh.

After a couple of shakes of his tail that had the same effect, he looked up, trying to gauge the time by the amount of light seeping down from the water's surface. The water was darker. That meant it was time for him to leave if he wanted to see the little fairy again without her knowing he was there.

Every night for the past week, the fairy who owned the rock shop in town made her way to the pool near Lovers' Lagoon. At least that's how long he'd been watching her. Quite by accident, he'd stumbled upon her   one evening after he'd taken a swim to quench his body's need for water. While he was lounging in the shallows of a pool fed by the lagoon, he'd heard a soft hum. The beauty of the voice lulled him, though not enough that he hadn't been able to shift quickly from his dragon form and hide himself in the shadows of the water's edge just before the voice's owner entered the pool area.

One thing was certain. He didn't want to miss out on seeing her again if he could. She was a fine-looking woman in her human form, but as a fairy... Kalen could practically feel his blood beginning to boil, not to mention other parts of his body starting to react. He tamped down his desire, not wanting to embarrass himself. It would be a whole lot harder to hide the visible signs of wanting her when he was in dragon form.

Mermaids called to him from where they had gathered near an old ship at the bottom of the harbor. Kalen ignored them and bid goodbye to the others who had shared his swim. He gave his tail two quick shakes, flattened his fins to his sides, and shot toward the surface. Shattering the water's crest, his form hurled into the air where he perfectly executed a lumbering spiral before diving back in and swimming toward the lagoon-fed pool. If her schedule held true, and most fairy's schedules were iron-clad, he'd make it back just in time.

Lounging in a darkened corner of the moonlit pool, Kalen listened. The sound of a soft song filled his head and his lips curved upward. Seconds later, his heartbeat hitched as the little pixie came into view.

He almost laughed at himself when he had to swallow a sigh so she wouldn't know he was there. He couldn't believe he was having such reactions to a woman... especially one who was clearly not a water dragon.

But this little water pixie managed to snag his attention in a way no other female had... at least not for a very long time. He almost sighed again, only the sound was interrupted by her giggle.

Kalen smiled. He leaned forward when she softly clapped her hands and reached down to scoop something out of the shallows. He squinted, trying to see what it was, but even with his exceptional eyesight, he couldn't tell. There must have been several more because she grabbed them up, more excited by each subsequent find.

When Kalen stretched forward, trying to get a better look, he lost his balance. The splash of his chest hitting the water caused the little fairy to freeze.

"Who's there?" the little pixie called out. Wide-eyed, she backed away from the water's edge, clutching her bag close to her as she glanced about. When Kalen didn't answer, she moved further into the surrounding woods, barely peeking out from behind a tree. Her gossamer wings fluttered, their motion jerky, nervous.

"Wait!" He called as she turned to run, but it was too late. Before he could climb out of the water, she'd lifted into the air and was gone.

Kalen cursed and began slogging toward the fallen log where he'd draped his clothes before his swim. He stopped when he realized he was at the spot where the fairy had found her treasure.

Glancing down, something caught his eye. Several somethings, actually. Just beneath the water's surface, a handful of colorful stones sparkled up at him. Frowning, he bent to scoop them up.

"Hearts?"

Kalen tried to remember what his aunt had told him about the shops along Sweet Street in Hernathea. They were all owned by fairies and angels, mostly related in some way or another, and each specialized in some form of love. His cousin had recently married the angel from the bakery. Her specialty was providing great cakes that somehow bound the couples together for eternity.

Or so they said.

There was a flower shop whose bridal bouquets were supposed to have some magical properties, a sandwich place with a special recipe for lovers, and a shop where a seer could tell all about future mates as well.

He shrugged. None of that had interested Kalen. It wasn't like he was looking for love.

Taking a couple of steps, he felt a warmth in his hands

that stopped him again. He stared down at the hearts, one of them practically glowing.

"What the…"

He turned the heart over in his hand and the warmth and glow faded. It must have been a trick of the light and his imagination. He shrugged again and moved to the log where he'd left his clothes.

Laying the hearts beside him, he didn't notice when the one that had glimmered slipped off into the grass below.

Chapter 2

Kalen might have no need for the magic the fairies and angels spun on Sweet Street, but he sure couldn't get that little water pixie out of his head throughout the night. Before he'd left the pool area, he'd rolled up his pant legs and grabbed the hem of his shirt so he could fill it with extra heart stones. He wasn't sure why she needed them, but her excitement when she'd found them had him wanting to make it up to her somehow. He figured he could take them to her. Maybe he'd score some brownie points.

Only, the more he'd thought about it through the night, the more he'd realized she wouldn't like it if she knew he'd been the one to see her. According to his aunt, the fairies were a cautious bunch. They didn't like anyone to catch them unaware in fairy form, especially those of a different species. One thing was certain, Kalen didn't want the rock shop owner to turn him away before she even gave him a chance.

With that in mind, he rolled out of bed, devising a new plan as he showered and readied for a quick trip into Hernathea. What he didn't understand was why his heart was behaving so strangely the whole time.

"Heart Stones, Harmony speaking. How may I help you?"

The phone had been ringing off the hook that morning and Harmony's nerves were about shattered. After almost a week of looking, last night, she'd finally found the magical heart stones. Only someone else was there at the pool as well and scared her off before she could gather more than a dozen.

Her heart plummeted into her stomach every time she thought of it. Not only had she been spotted by someone—maybe even by a human, but her precious heart stones... the stones she could only find twice a year... gone.

She had no idea what she was going to do. Those stones were the main staple of her business. The magic side, at least. As a leading Metaphysical Mineralogist, her skills at finding rare and precious stones were always in need. As long as people believed in the properties the minerals had to offer, she had nothing to worry about.

But in the magical realm, she was known for something more. Her heart stones were said to bind an individual with his or her true mate—the one the Universe had created just for them. And just twice a year, these special heart shaped stones washed ashore in a place only revealed to her.

That season, she'd been led to a secluded pool fed by Lovers' Lagoon on the East end of the island near Shaladorn Castle. When she'd found no stones the first couple of nights... because they had to be collected under magical moonlight... she believed maybe she'd misunderstood. But every evening when she meditated before the ruby heart, she'd heard the same thing. The instructions were clear... as clear as the large quartz stone that wowed customers from her window.

When the bell jingled letting her know someone had come into her shop, Harmony turned to give them the one-minute sign. She smiled politely and pointed to the phone, only when she saw the bag in his hand, she paused. Through the tan material, she could just make out the shape of a heart. Many hearts, actually.

"I'll get back with you," she told the person on the phone. Returning the handset to the receiver, she then went toward the man who had just walked into her shop, her eyes shifting from the bag in his hand to his face.

Brows drawn, head slightly cocked, she moved closer to him. "Can I help you, Mr. ...," she paused, hoping he would finish the sentence.

He didn't supply the answer right away, but he did smile, pulling her attention from the bag to focus fully on his face.

My oh my, what a face!

Blue-grey eyes with just a hint of green held an undercurrent of mischief within a face that looked as if the gods themselves had chiseled it—high, defined cheekbones and a sharp jawline leading to a neck that was ripe for kissing.

Harmony sucked in a sharp breath, hopeful he hadn't noticed, though his twitching lips told her he was well aware of her perusal. Even as her cheeks heated up, she couldn't keep her eyes from that mouth. Full lips framed straight, white teeth. A vision of passionate kisses and playful nips filled her head.

Enough!

She was being ridiculous. Besides, he had something she needed.

Of their own accord, her eyes swept to the waist of his fitted jeans, then dared to fall just below that line.

Oh, dear God, she thought. She needed to get this transaction over and him out the door or she was going to do something a good fairy shouldn't.

Turning her back on him, Harmony cleared her throat, trying to clear her head, and walked back toward her work area.

She motioned for him to follow, asking him again as they walked, what she could do for him.

Chapter 3

Kalen watched the little fairy's backside as she walked away. He quickly decided he had been wrong. She was every bit as hot in human form as she was with her wings fluttering. And since thoughts didn't lie, he knew the attraction was mutual.

He smiled. This little transaction might provide a bit more *action* than he'd anticipated.

"The stones in your bag, where in the world did you find them?"

Her words jarred him from thoughts of decadent adventures starring himself and the fairy. What was her name?

"I'm Harmony, by the way," she told him.

Kalen squinted, studying her for a moment while wondering whether she could read thoughts as well. Probably not. That wasn't something he'd ever heard fairies were known for.

She patted the table and he lifted the heavy bag, placing it in the middle. As he sat it down, the contents settled with a clinking tinkle, some of the hearts spilling out.

The little fairy's breath hitched when she saw the vast array. Reaching for one, a smallish blue-green stone, she held it gently and caressed the surface with her thumb. Replacing the first, she picked up another. The second was clearer, but with a hint of pink.

"Quartz?" he asked.

She nodded. "Rose quartz, actually. It's considered a *love stone*, and it's very popular for those trying to attract love or just to symbolize their love for the person it's given to. The first one I picked up was Amazonite. You have a lot of those, which is good."

She put the rose quartz down and picked up a couple of different blue-green stones in varying shades and sizes. "Amazonite is said to awaken the inner child. It inspires optimism and hope. They're popular, especially among my older clients." She shrugged and looked away, tucking a strand of her blonde hair behind her ear, her hand fluttering a bit before she turned back to the other hearts.

Kalen liked her enthusiasm and sensed her deep affection for the stones surrounding her. She seemed every bit as passioned about the stones as he was about his work. He watched her push through several different hearts before picking up one that was white with a spiral design in the center.

"That one reminds me of a seashell," he volunteered, causing her to jump since he'd moved closer to get a better look.

Harmony laughed. "It should. It's an operculum—the *trapdoor*, so to speak, for many snails. It's the part that closes when the soft part of the animal retracts. And when they die, they leave these little beauties behind for us to enjoy. Usually they're round. The heart-shaped ones are extra special."

"Ah! I've seen lots of those, then. I guess I just never

paid that much attention to them."

"Really?" She pulled her hand back and turned to look at him, cocking her head a bit, much like she had when he'd first come in.

Kalen tried to scan her thoughts and realized she had shuttered them.

Damn.

When he began to answer, stammering more than anything, she supplied the answer.

"You're a water dragon?"

"Yes," he answered, truthfully, holding his hand out after a couple of seconds. "Kalen Sikorsky," he said, finally introducing himself. "My father is Merdraak, the Sea King."

Harmony hesitated then took his hand ever so slowly and even without his ability to read her thoughts, he could sense her mental interrogation, asking him exactly where he was the night before.

She pulled her hand out of his and stood from the stool where she'd perched while they were looking. Taking a step back, she glanced from him to the partially spilled bag on her table.

"Where did you say you found these stones, Lord Sikorsky?"

Chapter 4

Kalen had never felt more like a dog trapped in a corner. He certainly didn't feel like a sea prince, though he'd come to expect that any time he came to Hernathea he would be on a more level playing field. His Herensuge cousins—the land dragons who lived in the castle that overlooked the town, were the *real royalty* of the island. His family was known, evidenced by the little fairy's response, but he was only one of many shifters. He knew if he spooked her, the fairy wouldn't hesitate to give him a boot right out of her shop.

All of this was suddenly going in a completely different direction than how he'd visualized it in his head. He thought of the plan he'd devised so that he could get the fairy the hearts without her knowing it was him who had been spying on her. He couldn't lie because that was impossible for his kind of dragon. But after her reaction, he couldn't risk her demanding he leave and him not ever getting the chance…

The chance for what?

He'd come to the shop, intending to pretend he'd found the bag of hearts so he could meet the fairy face-to-face, perhaps get a few *favors* as a show of her gratitude. But, now… Now, what did he want?

His heart pounding, his senses muddled, Kalen took a deep breath to tell her the complete truth.

"I, uh… they… they were… uhm…"

Kalen never had an issue with being at a loss for words, yet here in a matter of a few short minutes, it had happened to him twice. There was something about this woman that tied his tongue in all kinds of knots.

When she raised her eyebrows demanding an answer, he grimaced.

Wiping his palms on the sides of his jeans, Kalen took another deep breath.

"Out there," he blurted the words out with his breath. Turning ever so slightly, he motioned toward the outside of the shop in the direction of the pool where he'd found them.

"Out… there?" she asked, her head tilted as she looked at the front of the shop and then back at him.

Kalen nodded.

"Oh my! I wonder who left them? Did… did you see anyone when you came up, Mr. Sikorsky?"

Before he realized that she'd misunderstood him, Harmony rushed by him to the door of her shop, stopping only after she'd opened it and looked outside. Her brows were drawn when she shut the door and turned back toward him and spoke.

"Nobody. I suppose that's what you saw when you came in as well?"

Kalen nodded again. That part wasn't a lie. There hadn't been anyone. And, technically, he hadn't said someone else had left the stones. He simply hadn't corrected her assumptions. Not his fault, right?

Whispering a silent prayer of thanks to the Universe for covering his rear, Kalen stepped aside so the little fairy could return to her stool. He watched as she picked up another heart stone, her fingers gently stroking it as she turned it over in her hand.

Harmony absently played with the labradorite heart, oblivious to its flash and beauty. She was working hard to tamp down her disappointment. First, she'd felt a pull last night, an instant yearning when she entered the pool area. She'd ignored it because her need to find the stones was greater, but when she'd thought about it later, she'd felt almost certain it might be a connection to the person who'd been watching her.

And now Kalen Sikorsky was in her shop causing her to fight against such an intense attraction to him that she barely knew what to do with herself. From the minute he walked in, something inside her silently hoped he'd been the one at the pool... the one who'd found her hearts. The disappointment was tying her stomach into all kinds of knots.

If this water dragon wasn't the person who had been in the pool the night before, that meant there was someone else out there—some stranger that she'd been attracted to with such strength that it had to have been her chosen mate.

It sure would have made everything easier if the Sea Prince had been in that pool last night since he was sending her sense of attraction into overdrive as well. As it was, she really needed to find the other man if he really was *the one*.

She tapped the stones, her thoughts swirling like the lines within the operculum. She was so lost in her thoughts that she originally missed the water dragon's question. It wasn't until she'd already agreed to have dinner with him that she realized what he had said. And with her agreement secured, he'd quickly slipped out the door.

Finally managing to shut her mouth, Harmony stared at the door to her little gems and minerals shop. Oh, he was good, that one was. If only he had been *the one*, she thought for the hundredth time.

Chapter 5

Kalen wasn't exactly sure what had happened, but he walked out of Heart Stones & Diamonds a happy man. The little fairy had agreed to have an early dinner with him... though agreed might also have been fudging a bit. It was really more like she'd been distracted when he'd asked and had said yes before realizing what she'd said.

Regardless, he was going to see her again. Maybe, just maybe, the opportunity would come up and he could set the record straight. He'd tell her he was the one who had been at the pool, only he'd have to make sure she understood that he hadn't been spying. Not really. They simply happened to be in the same place at the same time. No one needed to know he'd high-tailed it back from his swim so he could be sure he was there where she couldn't see him just as he'd done for the past few nights.

Kalen cringed as he strolled away from the fairy's rock shop. His actions really did make him seem like the worst kind of creeper. He didn't know how, but somehow, some way he was going to get this whole thing straightened out. He put his hand over his heart and rubbed. If he was a betting man, he'd bet he had somehow begun to lose his heart. That wasn't a feeling he was used to at all.

With a sigh, Kalen slowed his pace, the scent of food reminding him he hadn't eaten breakfast. Two doors down, Dreamer's Deli was beckoning to him with the promise of satisfying even a water dragon's hunger. Too bad food wasn't all he was craving.

Creeper, he thought, as he opened the door to the little restaurant and stepped inside.

Harmony's forehead creased for the thousandth time since Kalen had left her shop. How in the world had she agreed to dinner with a man she barely knew?

Correction. She didn't barely know him. She didn't know him at all. They had just met. And yet she'd felt an instant connection to him, every bit as strong as the one she'd felt to the stranger at the pool. That one had startled her.

If she was being truthful, the reason she'd run from the pool was more out of fear of those feelings than anything else. That and, of course, not wanting to be seen by a human. But the more she thought about it, the less she worried her peeper had been human. She doubted a human would have held back in the shadows if he'd seen a fairy in her true form. Even in Hernathea where they mingled on a daily basis, they still seemed to get overly excited when one switched. Never would she ever have felt such a connection with a human.

Oh, there had been the occasional fairy-mortal marriage, but that was rare. Besides, as she'd thought before, for the feeling to have hit her so strongly, she couldn't help but feel the person was her chosen mate.

Her stomach flipped again. If the stranger was her true

mate and she'd let him get away... She shook her head. She was going to do whatever it took to find him. In fact, she planned to return to the pool after the sun went down. The moon may not be right for her to collect lovers' hearts, but that didn't matter. This time, the heart in question was her own, and maybe, just maybe, her mate would return as well. If he'd felt the same connection she had, he would surely try to find her.

Then again, had he not delivered the stones to her doorstep and run away?

With a frown, she turned her attention to the heart stones on the table in front of her. She sighed and shrugged and began sorting them. At least she hadn't had to carry the heavy bag back to her shop. Dumping the remaining hearts out of the bag, she stared in awe. She probably couldn't have carried it. Never in all her hundreds of years had she ever collected so many at one time.

Sorting through a few more of the heart stones, Harmony realized her attention was too scattered to really concentrate. Besides, her stomach had begun to growl. A quick glance at the heart-shaped clock on the wall told her the reason. It was almost eleven. Time for her to grab a sandwich from the deli down the way before their lunch crowd showed up. She'd need to hurry if she was going to make it. Dreamer's Deli was a favorite to townsfolks and tourists alike. It was legendary. Harmony chuckled as she flipped the *Be-Back-in-10-Minutes* sign on her front door.

All the little shops on Sweet Street were renowned, each one having a different hand in the act of finding and securing love. Too bad the angels and fairies didn't seem to be able to use the magic on themselves.

She thought about that as she strolled down the sidewalk. One of the stones *had* grown warm in her hand at the pool. Maybe she was wrong about the magic. Maybe that heart would be one of the ones in the bag waiting for her on the worktable in her shop and both of them would have handled it.

Harmony smiled at the thought as she pulled open the door of the deli, though the jovial moment quickly passed when she saw her cousin Desi talking with the water dragon. She loved her cousin, but if there was anyone who could be labeled as a big flirt, it was definitely Desi. There was something about the saucy redhead that drew men to her like a moth to a flaming candle.

Laughing at something the water dragon had said, Desi smiled and waved at her. Harmony forced her lips to curve upward and gave a little finger wiggle as she moved up to the counter.

"Harmony! Hi!"

A young woman appearing to be around the same age as she and her cousin came through a door that led to the food prep area of the deli. Harmony knew that's what was back there because she'd visited the deli a few times outside of regular business hours.

The woman moving toward her was an angel— Cassandra Sweet. She owned Dreamer's Deli and her father just happened to be the man who owned the buildings that housed the little shops up and down Sweet Street. Cassie had built the deli into what it was without her father's help, though. She used to laugh and say she paid her rent just like everyone else.

Harmony gave her order and then glanced over her shoulder before turning her attention back to the angel. She watched as Cassie cut her big blue eyes in the direction of the red-haired fairy and the water dragon. The woman, whose hair was not quite as blonde as hers, raised an eyebrow in question when she looked back.

"He's one of the Herensuge's cousins," Harmony offered. "There seems to be a new one crawl into town every other day."

The two women chuckled, and Cassie added that at least they were nice to look at.

Harmony agreed, though her smile was starting to fade again. Desi's laughter told her that her cousin thought so, too.

It didn't matter, she reminded herself. Later, when she went back to the pool, she would find her mate. It really should be him causing her stomach to flutter, not the water dragon flirting with her cousin.

With a disgruntled huff, she took her order and told Cassie goodbye. She turned to leave, hopeful she would get away with a simple wave in Desi's direction. No such luck. She tapped her watch indicating she needed to get back, but Desi held up the one-minute finger and motioned her over.

"Harmony!" The redhead stood and hugged her cousin. "You simply have to meet Kalen. He's one of the Herensuges. Well, a Sikorsky, actually, but... a water dragon. Can you believe that?"

Harmony pasted on a smile. "You don't say?"

"Ms. Heartstone and I have already had the pleasure," Kalen chuckled.

"Really?"

Desi's excitement surprised Harmony because her cousin was always on the prowl and jealous of any who moved into her way. In light of this, Harmony's own jealousy left her feeling a bit catty.

Tapping her cousin's shoulder with her own, the petite blonde fairy told her that she really did have to get going, that she'd left her shop unattended to grab lunch. She lifted her sandwich and drink a bit higher as if she needed to offer proof.

"I really need to be getting back to work as well," Desi offered, glancing around at the increasing number of people filing in.

She worked for Cassie. They had been best friends since they were little and when Cassie's boyfriend left her to manage the deli alone, Desi had stepped in.

Harmony felt remorse for her irritation toward her cousin. Desi really wasn't a bad person. In fact, she helped a lot of people in different ways. She was a seer and her special gift was reading stones to help direct people along the right paths, especially those paths that would lead them to their one true love.

Her advice to Harmony when she'd read hers was to continue what she was doing, and love would find her.

Harmony thought of the mystery person in the pool. Was that what she'd meant?

She felt eyes on her, and Harmony realized she'd been

so lost in her thoughts that she'd missed whatever had been said. She gave herself a mental shake.

"I'm sorry, I…"

"You were a million miles away there for a moment," Kalen supplied.

He smiled that infectious smile again and Harmony was hit anew with his handsomeness. The sudden draw of attraction washed over her, and she wondered again why he couldn't have been the person at the pool.

She almost groaned and then caught herself.

"I'd better get going," she said quietly.

Kalen unfolded his tall form from the chair. "Looks like my lunch is ready as well." He reached for Desi's hand and shook it. "It was nice to see you again, Desi. Thanks for your advice." He turned to Harmony, "I'll stop by around four," he told her.

Since her hands were full, he patted her upper arm, letting his hand linger for a moment longer than necessary before she pulled away.

Breathe, Harmony told herself as she gazed into his pale sea glass blue eyes. She blinked. Had his eyes not been blue-grey with a hint of green earlier?

She muttered goodbye and turned to leave. She was still lost in thoughts of his eyes, wondering if maybe they changed, just like the sea.

Only she wasn't too lost in her thoughts to overhear her cousin.

"So, that's why you needed to know a good place to eat here in town. And here I thought you were just hitting on me."

Harmony rolled her eyes at Desi's flirtatious laughter. At least she knew her cousin well enough to know the other woman was no threat to her now that she knew Kalen's plans.

She frowned. Maybe that wasn't such a fair deal for the sea dragon. After all, if she was able to find the other man…

She only hoped he would make her heart do half as many flips as it did in Kalen's presence.

Why must life present so many forks in the road without none being the clear-cut path? That seemed to be the way with all big decisions.

If her hands hadn't been full, she just might have shaken her fist at the Universe.

Chapter 6

The afternoon flew by. Harmony sorted through the remainder of the heart stones, placing phone calls to let several other dealers know what she had as well as filling orders for those who had already contacted her. Before she knew it, her alarm sounded, alerting her that she needed to take a few minutes to freshen up before dinner with the water dragon.

She really needed to stop calling him that and think of him by his name.

"Kalen," she said, trying it out. She smiled, liking the way it felt on her tongue. She tried it again and giggled when she wondered if he tasted as good as his name felt. That thought made her cheeks flame and she rolled her eyes.

You'd think as a fairy who specialized in bringing lovers together with her heart stones, she'd be more versed in the subject. But on a personal level... she sighed. In her couple hundred years, there'd been no one special. She'd never minded... until now.

Harmony wiped her hands on a paper towel she wheeled off the roll in her shop bathroom and swallowed hard as she looked in the mirror. Accepting this date had been a mistake.

Her reflection shook her head back at her. At least someone thought they were doing the right thing!

The bell on her door jingled and she looked at her clock. She had to hand it to the sea dragon. If nothing else, the man was punctual. Pressing her lips together to evenly distribute the lipstick she'd just put on, Harmony smiled at her reflection and turned to greet her date.

It's just dinner, she reminded herself. That thought went out the window when she looked up and saw him standing in her shop, a handful of flowers and a heart-shaped box in his hands.

She frowned and he laughed.

"You're supposed to be impressed," he chuckled before moving forward and handing her the box. "It's rocks!"

"Rocks?"

Kalen nodded. "It was your cousin's idea. Well, I mean I thought of the rocks, but she came up with the heart box. I thought it was pretty inventive. Much better than chocolates." He smiled sheepishly moving up beside Harmony when she set the box on the table.

"It really is a fun idea," she assured as she lifted the lid.

She gasped and looked from the contents to the water dragon and then back again.

"Where... how in the world did you get these?" she practically whispered.

Kalen leaned forward and peered in the box. He frowned. "That bad?"

Harmony looked at him expecting him to crack a smile letting her know he was joking, only she saw genuine concern.

"The majority of the stones in here are rare and very valuable. They're... beautiful, but... I really can't accept them." She stopped just short of telling him the heart shaped box had been on the verge of too much for a first date, but the gems... definitely not something you gave to someone you just met.

Kalen's forehead wrinkled as his frown deepened. He looked at the contents of the box again and then back at Harmony. How could the stones be rare when they were easily found along the bottom of the sea? He tried to probe her mind to no avail.

Stroking his chin, Kalen watched as she replaced the top of the box and slid it toward him. He could tell the few minutes of silence was going to grow awkward. He needed to say something and yet he was still trying to come to terms with what had just happened. When he'd run his idea for the stones across Desi, she'd told him to find stones from his world beneath the sea...

"Oh!" he exclaimed, making Harmony jump. He laughed and she frowned, which made him laugh again. "I get it. These stones... I didn't realize they were rare up here. On the seabed, I can find them easily."

"You can?"

The way she scrunched her nose made Kalen momentarily regret what he'd said. Yes, they were plentiful, but he had taken the time to go to a spot where he knew they would be available and had hand-picked each one. It wasn't a thoughtless, grab-a-handful-and-go gift.

"You have to know where to find them, but... yes..."

He reached for the box and removed the lid. Lifting one stone, he held it up to her and raised an eyebrow in question.

"That one is ocean jasper. There's only one ocean-facing mine where you can find it, it's in Madagascar. It's pretty unique—mined exclusively by women running their own business in that country."

Kalen was impressed. He hadn't known that. What he did know is there were several deposits of it within his reach. One was on a beach along the backside of his family's castle, though he'd found this one much closer to Hernathea.

He replaced the ocean jasper and picked up another. It was clear and shiny. Well, shiny in spots.

"That's a Herkimer diamond."

She laughed when his mouth rounded in surprise.

"It's not a *real* diamond and not quite as rare as the others, though they're found mostly only around Herkimer County, New York. It's a double terminated quartz, actually. They're one of my favorites. They're the most powerful of all the quartz crystals."

She reached for the tiny crystal, her fingers barely caressing his in the process. Kalen swallowed hard, fighting against an intense desire to touch her again. Had she stared into his eyes a second longer, he was sure his hand would have risen of its own accord to stroke the softness of her ivory cheek.

But she had looked away, refocusing on the little gem in her hand. She'd shivered slightly before continuing to speak.

"The points on each end," she spoke softly. "Allows them to not only transmit their own energies, but to receive spiritual energy and to amplify and focus it intently. That makes them desirable."

"Desirable," he said. His voice was a bit husky and the little fairy tittered nervously. He cleared his throat and reached for another stone—a blue one.

"That's Larimar. It's a variety of a mineral called Pectolite which, in and of itself, isn't rare. But the blue colored Larimar is. It's found only in the Dominican Republic and is the only gemstone found in the entire Caribbean."

She put down the Herkimer she was still holding and turned to him. "So do you see why I was surprised?" She waved her hand toward the box. "Most of these are found in one place in the world and you're telling me they're common stones in your world. It was a shock."

Kalen laughed and put the Larimar back in the box.

"I hope you'll reconsider keeping them. I did spend the afternoon gathering them, so hopefully that makes them somewhat special all the same." As if on cue, his stomach grumbled.

Harmony chuckled. "It sounds like you worked up quite a hunger from all that hard work." She replaced the lid on the box and slipped off her stool. "Let me just put this up for safe keeping and we can be on our way. Where did Desi recommend for dinner?" she asked as she walked over to a large cabinet, stopping to fish a key out of her handbag.

Kalen was pleased that she seemed nonplused that he'd asked her cousin for help. He was concerned when she'd walked into the deli earlier that day and he'd been sitting with the redhead, especially since Desi seemed to be flirting a bit. He'd known from scanning her thoughts that was just her nature. Besides, he'd also met her before when she'd attended a party at his family's castle with one of his younger brothers. That in itself made her off limits, even if the relationship had never taken hold. There was still a code of expected conduct among brothers.

Thoughts of the red headed fairy quickly left him as the petite blonde walked back toward him. He reached for the light jacket she'd left on the table and held it up so she could slip into it. He wondered if she'd noticed his hesitation in releasing her once he'd helped her situate the material over her shoulders. He couldn't resist leaning into her and breathing deeply, knowing she'd smell of a Spring meadow mixed with a lovely sea breeze. He wasn't disappointed.

Stepping to the side, she turned slightly, smiling up at him before taking the arm he offered and sweeping her hand out indicating he should lead the way.

He chuckled, realizing he hadn't answered her question when she'd asked where they were going. The little fairy had absolutely no idea of what he had in store.

Chapter 7

Harmony was glad to be beside the sea dragon instead of behind him. She knew, without a doubt, that his backside, shaped by the soft stretch of his high dollar cotton chinos, would have been an amazing distraction.

As it was, heat seeped through the sleeve of his sea blue polo where her hand lay against his arm, causing a warmth in places it probably shouldn't have. It wasn't even as if the tightness of the shirt was indecent, but it was enough to show off the definition of his muscles. The light ripple beneath her fingers told her this man was beyond fit, perhaps too much so for her soft fairy body. Then again, he had been the one to ask her to dinner.

Harmony's thoughts flew to a vision of their bodies intertwined. Hard against soft, tan melting into pale... She was glad he wasn't looking at her at that moment because she could feel her cheeks coloring and she certainly didn't want to have to try to explain. At least since she knew he was a dragon she'd been quick-witted enough to shutter her thoughts. Otherwise, he would surely already know exactly what she was thinking.

That thought made her shudder and he looked down at her, his sexy smile doing nothing to alleviate the ache that had begun growing inside her.

How easy it would be to get lost in those eyes that were currently the color of the sea just before sunset. She could almost feel the light scratch of his five o'clock shadow against her neck, her belly, the inside of her thigh... She imagined her hands in his hair that was almost as long as her own. She wondered how she had missed that fact of him then realized this was the first time she'd seen him with it loose. She liked it. It fit him.

Blessed hair, she thought, thankful it had pulled her out of her wanton thoughts. The desire was still there, but at least her control had returned.

She was also thankful this was an early date. She'd already told him she had a prior engagement later, which was the reason they were going early. What she hadn't mentioned was her plan to return to the pool once the moon had risen. It wouldn't be a magical moon, so any stones she found would be just that... simple heart stones. But the person who had seen her the night before, the one who had brought the hearts to her shop, wouldn't know that. She had to try to find him.

And if she couldn't... she gave Kalen's arm a light squeeze. The idea of not pursuing the sexy sea dragon was quickly starting to seem absurd.

Chapter 8

Kalen could tell the little fairy was impressed when he led her to his Bentley convertible sitting in the parking lot at the end of the street. Like most of the streets in the magical district, Sweet Street was open to foot traffic only.

In part, that created a bit of old-fashioned nostalgia for anyone walking through. It also had the added advantage of slowing down potential shoppers, increasing their interest as they took the time to look into the windows of the shops instead of whizzing on by at the break-neck speed of the rest of the world.

Kalen had to admit, though, that even Hernathea seemed fast compared to the smaller island that housed his family's castle and little more. Granted, most of what they did took place beneath the water's surface, but still. Even down below, the pace seemed much more leisurely.

As he helped her into the car, Kalen had the sudden desire to show his world to Harmony. He was proud of his heritage, of what his family built. Their research into the medicinal uses of aquatic plant life had been helping mystical beings for centuries. Many of the current formulas had evolved from ancient remedies while others were brand new. They'd even recently come up with a formula that would increase the life span of mortal mates of mystic beings. It hadn't been perfected where immortality was attainable, but a couple hundred extra years with someone loved was a lot better than the potential seventy to eighty years of most humans. And that was barring disease of any kind.

Kalen shivered. His people easily lived ten times that, and it seemed too short. A vision of hundreds of years rolling by filled his head. He'd take them, especially if they were filled with Harmony by his side.

He glanced over at the fairy and almost sighed. He had no idea how, but he swore she looked more beautiful every time he saw her.

Harmony sat up straighter as they passed by the last signs of civilization. She'd felt no hint of a check that would have told her to be cautious of the man, but... leaving the confines of Hernathea hadn't crossed her mind either.

A low chuckle pulled her attention to the dragon shifter sitting in the driver's seat and she turned questioning eyes to him.

"It's a surprise, but don't worry. Other people will be there as well."

He laughed, tapping his hand against the steering wheel when she opened her mouth and no words came out.

"There's a private beach just a few miles up the road here. I've had a meal catered for us from your chameleon friend's restaurant. Desi said it was one of your favorites."

Harmony nodded slowly. That's really where she'd expected him to take her.

"I did ask some of the staff from Shaladorn to help out

since *Changes* will be gearing up for their dinner hour. I hope it's okay. I think it'll be fun." He cocked a hopeful brow.

Harmony tried to reassure him with a smile.

Fun? How could it not be?

It was one of the many items on her bucket list—a romantic dinner on a private beach with a drop-dead gorgeous man. She looked at him from the corner of her eye. There was no way he had gotten that bit of info in the short time before she'd shuttered her thoughts after realizing he had a dragon's uncanny ability to read minds.

Desi.

That was the only answer. He didn't need to read her mind when he had her cousin on his side. That little matchmaker wannabe had told him all her secret desires! She was so going to get her. Or thank her with the world's biggest hug. Harmony wasn't quite sure which, yet.

Kalen steered the car off to the side of the road just as another vehicle appeared through the brush. Dark sea blue in color, it looked something like a modified golf cart but longer in length to provide extra legroom in the back seat that faced forward. Harmony noted that it seemed to have more appropriate tires and better suspension.

"Your beach buggy awaits, my lady," Kalen joked as he got out and came around to open her door.

Harmony smiled up at him as he offered his hand to help her out of the car. It appeared he'd thought of everything. One thing was certain, she'd never had a guy go to so much trouble to impress her. The thought made her stomach flutter and she had to fight off a shiver as he led her to the buggy.

The man in the front passenger seat jumped out and pulled back some brush to reveal a sandy path.

Impressive.

Harmony jumped slightly when Kalen tossed his car keys to the man holding the brush and told him to be careful. The man mock saluted and let the bushes fall back into place, cutting them off as they ventured into a part of her world she'd never even known was there.

They both chuckled as the vehicle made its way along the path, the unevenness of the sand causing them to bump together.

"Your family owns this beach?" she asked after a few minutes of neither of them talking.

Kalen nodded, then shook his head. "Yes and no. It's in the family, but actually part of the Shaladorn grounds which will be passed down through my uncle's line. The castle's not too far up the road. It takes a bit longer to get there by car than it does the water."

Harmony smiled. "I've been there a few times. Mrs. Herensuge has an extensive *rock* garden, as she calls it." They both laughed. "Desi and I worked on it together and add to it from time to time. I guess you could say it's our job to make sure it has just the right pieces to keep peace and prosperity flowing into the castle and its inhabitants."

She shrugged and looked down. While she loved what she did, it was a bit embarrassing to talk about at times. Not everyone believed in the metaphysical properties of her stones.

Her stones. Ha! Back in the sixteenth century when she was working under Bauer, he cautioned her about taking ownership of the *subjects with which she worked*. She snorted lightly. He may have been later dubbed the Father of Mineralogy, but early mineralogists had a much better grasp on the aspects of the inner good and beauty of the stones.

"I didn't realize you had a hand in creating Aunt Michial's mineral garden! It's truly beautiful. Some of the pieces are quite unique. Maybe some time, you can tell me more about them."

Harmony felt her heart swell. She'd had people feign interest in what she did or in the stones themselves in their attempt to get closer to her, but she sensed a genuine desire for knowledge in Kalen's request.

She'd noticed the same when she'd told him about some of the different heart stones and again when they'd been discussing the pieces in the heart shaped box he'd given to her. This water dragon was either one smooth character or practically perfect. Harmony sure hoped it was the second, though perfect was going to be that much harder to walk away from.

Stop, she told herself. The date had barely started and here she was already thinking about the end.

Uncertainty gnawed at her insides again, forcing her to push it away as they cleared the bushes and came out onto a bare stretch of beach. Down the way, she could make out the flicker of light and hear the faint sound of soft music. The chords were gentle and romantic, just like the lap of the waves not too many feet away. Harmony swallowed a chuckle. She'd heard plenty of waves before. These were romantic because of the man that sat beside her. She smiled and turned her head, noticing he was watching her.

"Do you like it?" he asked, his voice quiet, hopeful.

Harmony nodded, reaching up to push a strand of hair back that had whipped loose in the ocean breeze.

"It's... stunning." She turned to look again at the water and back up to the quickly approaching scene before looking back at him.

"Yes, it is."

Harmony gulped. He was looking only at her.

She knew it was cliché, but she couldn't help the feeling that time around them stood still. It was as if a bubble encapsulated them and the rest of the world disappeared, especially when he glanced down at her lips, his eyes asking permission when they locked again with hers.

Harmony's breathing slowed and her core tightened when she felt his fingers encircle hers. When his right arm wrapped around her shoulders, she tipped her head up, leaning into him ever so slightly.

Don't do this.

The thought was brief, fleeting. She knew she shouldn't let him kiss her since she had plans later to meet someone else, but damned if she couldn't help herself. At that moment, she wanted nothing more than to feel his mouth on hers. She wanted to be scorched by that heat and deal with the aftermath later. It was just a kiss. Kissing meant nothing...

Was that why she was so nervous?

Kalen barely brushed his lips over hers before pulling away. Harmony's eyes popped open, shock and bewilderment forcing her to blink several times.

"We're here," he whispered, releasing her as if nothing remotely intimate and lifechanging had been about to happen between them.

Harmony's brows inched toward her hairline before coming back down, only slightly lower than they were. Inexperienced or not, there was no way she could have misread his intent. Kalen Sikorsky had been about to kiss her and now she was watching his backside as he slipped out of the cart before turning to offer her his hand.

Schooling her features in an attempt to hide her disappointment, Harmony slipped her fingers inside his, almost hating how the warmth of his hand turned her insides to mush. By the time he walked her the short distance to the already set table, she had forgiven him, especially when the spread included so many of her favorite *Chameleon* dishes.

"You really went to a lot of trouble," she told him after thanking him for seating her and watching him move around to take his place on the opposite side of the table.

Kalen smiled and shrugged. "To be honest, it's been a lot of fun planning and plotting to bring everything together in such a short time."

He nodded to the gentleman in a suit with a napkin over his arm. When the man showed him a bottle of wine, Kalen nodded and the man poured each a glass and stepped away, disappearing into the shadows, leaving them seemingly alone.

"Well, you did a great job. And you even had time for

a swim." She was referring to the box of precious stones he'd collected for her.

Kalen had just taken a bite of food from his plate and gave her the one-minute sign, indicating he needed to finish his bite. "Speaking of… you'll never believe what I found while I was under." When Harmony shook her head, he continued. "A sheltered grove filled with Callitriche pulchra."

Harmony knew by the excited pitch of his voice that she should be as thrilled with his find as he was, but the name had absolutely no meaning to her.

Seeing her confusion, Kalen tried to explain.

"It's a plant thought to be located only on Gavdos Island, near Crete. And even there, its numbers have been dwindling, thanks to tourism and all."

"And you found some near here?" Knowing how she felt about rare mineral finds, Harmony could finally share in his excitement.

"I did!" He nodded.

"That's fantastic! Your family has done amazing things for the medical field where aquatic plants are concerned. I don't know that our kind would still be around if it weren't for the diligence of your ancestors."

Now it was Kalen's turn to blush a bit. "I can't really take credit for what they did before me, but I will damned sure do my best to see that it's carried on."

"I'm glad," she told him. "There's such a need, especially as our worlds mingle more and more with the mortals. Too many are leaving the old ways… I mean, I'm all for modern conveniences, but there's balance, you know?"

Kalen nodded and they spent the rest of the meal discussing old and new ways, talking a lot about their ancestors and how each came to do what they did.

Harmony took one last bite of her salted caramel-filled molten chocolate cake and dropped her fork onto her plate.

"This meal has been delicious, but I think if I eat another bite, I'm going to pop!" She pushed herself back from the table just a bit. "As it is, I don't think my fairy could fly, even if she had to."

They both laughed and Kalen took one more bite before following suit. He stood and walked around the table taking her elbow as she began to stand.

"The sun will be setting soon. How about a short stroll before you have to leave?"

Harmony's heart plummeted. She didn't want to think about leaving. What she really wanted was to tell him she'd rather stay, to watch the sunset with him followed by a sleepless night greeted by tomorrow's sunrise. Instead she nodded and slipped her arm into his as they made their way toward the waves.

By the time they'd reached the firmer sand closer to the water, their hands were intertwined, swinging between them. Kalen turned them so they would be walking in the direction where they'd come onto the beach. Neither spoke at first as they walked, both enjoying the salty breeze.

"There's no clearer water anywhere on Earth," Kalen smiled at his volunteered information.

"Have you been everywhere?" she teased.

The sea dragon shook his head. "Not yet, but can you imagine there is?"

Harmony laughed. "If only life was that simple. If only we could imagine, and it would be so."

Kalen stopped abruptly and twirled her around, bringing her close. He dipped his head and kissed her, still briefly, though filled with potential promise. "I wanted to do that earlier, but then we were getting so close to the others… I didn't want to make you feel uncomfortable."

Harmony nodded wondering how she'd managed to find this man—this perfect gentleman. He was everything she could ever have imagined. She wished she could tell him that, wanted to let him know she would stay. But she couldn't. She could barely breathe, let alone speak. Especially when all she wanted was for him to kiss her again… To kiss her in a way that would quench the longing she'd felt since…

Since the night before when she'd run from the pond.

She looked down, her forehead resting on his chest.

Kalen slipped a hand beneath her chin and coaxed her to look up at him. He could tell she wanted him every bit as much as he wanted her. Her posture was rigid while she gauged his next move, the way she wet her lips when his gaze dropped to them… it all gave her away, and when he leaned forward, she gasped quietly.

Everything about her indicated she'd stay if he just asked. He could have her just this once, and then walk away so that she would be free to find her future. He could... if he wanted to spend the rest of his life trying to repair the hole left in his heart.

Self-preservation kicked in and he patted her arm as he stepped away and lifted his hand into the air. A snap of his fingers brought the gentle purr of a small engine and the same cart that had delivered them to the beach appeared from a hidden path.

"I've asked Remey to take you back," he told her as the man on the cart stopped next to them. "I thought it might be easier this way."

Kalen turned to look out at the water, a sad smile playing on his lips. "You'd better get going," he whispered without looking back at her. "You don't want to be late."

Chapter 9

Harmony wasn't sure heartbreak could happen after knowing someone for such a short time, but if it could, she was pretty sure hers was shattering into a million pieces as she stared at the back of the sea dragon. She was oblivious to the brilliance of the sunset glistening on the water beyond where he stood.

"Miss?"

The driver's voice pulled her away from the vision and, after a few more seconds, she turned and followed him to the cart. She was thankful they were already at the exit path for the private beach, because sitting alone for any length of time in that seat might have had her jumping from the cart so she could run back and tell Kalen she was wrong. She wanted to tell him he was her future, not some fantasy person that may or may not be real.

What an idiot, she thought as the other man pulled back the bushes and they drove through.

Don't do this. It's not too late, her inner voice told her as he helped her into the back of a fancy car just shy of an outright limo.

But it *was* too late. In fact, it had been too late even before it had begun. Knowing her mate was out there, that she'd run from him the night before, she should never have agreed to see the sea dragon at all.

Harmony sat in the back seat of the car her head lolled

back against the soft leather. At that moment, she felt completely, devastatingly alone and knew Kalen had been right to send her on her own. There was never anything easy about saying goodbye.

Chapter 10

By the time they arrived at her little house, the numbness had settled in enough for Harmony to at least pass as a functioning individual. She thanked the driver and let herself into the cottage by the pond that had once belonged to her great grandmother. She's the one who had taught Harmony how to swim as opposed to just skimming along the water's surface, like most water pixie fairies.

"There's a whole other world down there, my little harbinger of love. Someday, you might want to explore it."

"Someday," Harmony whispered into the quiet cottage as she stumbled inside, tears clouding her vision. She blinked them away and shook her head.

This had been her choice. She had to find out if the stone had warmed because the man at the pool was her chosen mate, her future.

"Please," she whispered looking up. "Let him be there so I'll know and can get on with my life."

She hated the uncertainty, hated the thought that Kalen might be hurting every bit as much as she was if not more. At least she had the possibility of finding her mate as the alternative. What would he get besides knowing he wasn't the one?

How ironic, she thought. Situations like this were the very reason her magical heart stones were in such high demand. The knowledge one of them could reveal could save an awful lot of heartache.

She sighed. She was doing the right thing. She was, and after tonight, she'd be absolutely sure because her future was waiting for her at that pool. She just knew it.

Too bad absolute had very little place when it came to love.

Chapter 11

Harmony tried hard to replicate the past few nights. She didn't pray for revelation from the great ruby stone, but everything else was the same. She went to the pond fed by the lagoon at the exact same time, hummed the tune she always hummed, and even fluttered along the path she'd taken the night before.

Everything was perfect, she thought, as she lit beside the water, peering into the shadows that surrounded her for a brief moment before she started to walk along the shallow edge looking for stones.

There were a fairly decent number of new heart stones that had washed to the shallows, along with other stones that she picked up. Harmony didn't just sell the heart shaped favorites. She had an equal number of clients looking for other pieces. Most she purchased, but a good number she found herself, especially the hearts and always the magical ones.

She picked up a few more stones, skipping a couple of them across the water's surface before looking around again. There was no one there.

She sighed. Whoever had been there the other night wasn't coming back. She'd never know who it was or if he truly was her chosen one. All because she'd been too afraid.

Just like she'd been with Kalen.

That was the truth. She'd left because she was afraid.

And, now what? Was he gone to her, too?

While she thought things over, Harmony made her way to a large log that lay just beyond the shallows of the pool. She laid the stones she'd picked up on it then climbed up beside them. Why did everything have to be so hard all of a sudden? A few days ago, she'd been just fine. She'd been having trouble finding her heart stones, but otherwise, life had been sailing along as easy as always. And now...

A noise in the distance caught her attention. It sounded like a splash from something mighty big falling.

Sliding off the log, Harmony began to flit her way toward the lagoon that fed the pond where she'd been looking. She had no idea what, but something was going on. Hopefully she wouldn't embarrass herself and come across a group of lovers. It was known as Lovers' Lagoon, after all.

Chapter 12

The splashing continued, though Harmony quickly realized it wasn't in the lagoon. She followed the water and ended up on a beach about half a mile away. Only as she got closer could she see what was causing all the ruckus. It was the splash of a very large sea dragon as he lunged himself out of the water, performing acrobatic moves any diver would be proud of before plunging back into the water. On the shore, a handful of seals clapped each time, barking their appreciation and encouragement. They looked young, giggling before scurrying back into the water as she came closer.

They must have met the sea dragon beneath the surface and let him know someone else had arrived because he broke the surface barely making a sound in the moonlight. He keyed in on her location almost immediately.

"Hey!" she called, waving.

He bobbed to his side and waved a fin at her.

"What are you doing here?" he asked as he swam as close as he could without leaving the water and dwarfing her with his size.

Harmony waded out part way, so they'd be closer.

She shrugged. "My plans sort of fell through, so…" She shrugged again and he stared at her for a few seconds before nodding. She got the distinct feeling he was assessing her, scrutinizing the truth in her statement. She didn't mind. She would have done the same.

"Well, since you're here, wanna go for a swim? The water's really warm tonight. Gotta take advantage of it before the winter chills start setting in."

Harmony shivered. She didn't want to think about winter, even though it was one of her biggest times of the year for sales. Hearts and winter holidays sort of went together.

After a few minutes, she nodded. "Sure, why not? But you'll have to give me a minute. I don't breathe under water the way you do. My, uh... my lungs have to..." She wasn't sure if she wanted to finish the sentence. Some beings were seriously uncomfortable with the idea.

"Fill with water?" he finished for her and she nodded. "It's not too different for me, it just happens without me even thinking about it, I guess. Probably because I've been doing it my whole life."

They both laughed.

"Well, I have to ease into it. It's not instantaneous and some people think it's gross."

"Good thing we're not *some people*, then." They both laughed again, and he began to back up and turn around. "I'll just, uh... I'll wait over there." He tipped his head toward a spot where a piece of driftwood bobbed in the water. "If you need anything..."

"I just need you to go!" She laughed at his feigned hurt and waited for him to swim the short distance away before she began to wade deeper into the water.

"Here goes," she whispered to herself as she took a deep breath and submerged herself fully. The saltwater stung her eyes for only a minute before they adjusted. She remembered swimming beneath the surface of the sea with her great grandmother a few times so she knew she could do it. She'd told her to just take it slow, especially when it had been a while since she'd been in the water.

Harmony concentrated on blowing out small amounts of the air in her lungs while taking in water. When her body began to fight the process, she forced herself to relax, allowing the two to mix until there was finally more water than air and she was breathing easily. She smiled as she looked around, excited to enjoy the beauty of the depths with someone else who appreciated it as much as she did. She hadn't had that since her great grandmother had passed.

Pushing a fleeting moment of sadness out of her mind, she got her bearings and swam toward the bulky form of the sea dragon.

When she was almost there, he ducked his head beneath the surface and smiled at her, making her laugh. It wasn't that he was funny looking or anything, just that seeing him in his dragon form was so new and different, and yet he felt like Kalen. He *was* Kalen. And he was beautiful, really.

Unlike most of the land dragons she'd met, Kalen didn't have scales. His skin more closely resembled the smooth surface of a whale or dolphin. He was distinctly blue—darker on the top, fading to a lighter, almost white, on the bottom. His flippers were similar to those of his seal friends, though he had four instead of two, and his tail was long, ending in a forked fluke. At the top of his neck, beneath his horned head, frilled flaps overlapped adding to his majestic look. She couldn't wait to see him moving through the water.

As if he'd read her mind, Kalen dove beneath her, twisting and turning as he sliced through the water before rolling onto his back and motioning for her to follow. Harmony stretched her arms over her head and used her legs and wings to maneuver toward the water giant. She knew he'd have to slow his pace so that she could keep up, but at least since she was a true water fairy, she had the ability to go faster than a human, thanks to her wings that acted as a propeller.

Kalen looked her over and Harmony could tell he was assessing how well she was doing beneath the water. When he was satisfied she was okay, he started to swim farther away from the shore. Harmony had no idea where they were going, but her instincts told her to trust him, that he'd keep her safe.

They hadn't gone very far when an old ruin came into view and Harmony could feel her heartbeat escalating with excitement. Massive pillars covered in marine plant life rose from the silt, plants, and debris on the sea floor. Fish in varying sizes and colors swam around, through what used to be elaborate windows, the glass vanishing long ago.

Palms up, Harmony shrugged, hopeful Kalen would figure out she was wondering what the ruin had been. She hadn't always lived in Hernathea so there was a lot about the history she didn't know. If she had to guess, she'd say the place must have been overtaken by the sea centuries before.

Kalen squinted at her, the near-humanness of his action

causing her to chuckle, though when he closed his eyes, she could feel him probing her mind. She fidgeted for a minute or two when he popped one eye open to look at her. Harmony wasn't quite sure she wanted him in her head.

Then it dawned on her. That was the only way they could communicate below the surface. Reluctantly, she unshuttered her mind, hearing him almost immediately when she did.

"Thank you! I promise I won't probe deeper, but this way we can talk," he told her… or more, he thought to her.

Harmony nodded, suddenly at a loss for words until an eel swam by and she remembered exactly where they were.

Kalen laughed. "Don't worry. That's the non-stinging kind," he assured.

Pretending to wipe sweat from her brow, Harmony turned back to the ruin. "What is, or was this place? It's beautiful."

Easing through one of the doors that was large enough for his massive body, Kalen took her into the most intact part of the ruin. Inside, it was easy to see they were in part of a chapel. The stone altar still stood on a raised dais along what one would assume was the front wall. A sculpture of a faceless deity hung on the wall above it with long, narrow glassless windows on either side. They would have let in light once upon a time, though now they merely served as doorways for smaller fish. When she noticed mounds of debris running the width of the room, she looked at Kalen, her brows going down.

"They used to be pews," he told her. "When I first discovered this place, there were more walls and a few roofs, even. The pews were semi-intact as well, though the water over the years has broken down the wood and rusted any metal. The stone is about all that remains."

Harmony could feel a wave of sadness rush over him.

"At least we can still enjoy the beauty of what's left," she thought softly.

Kalen nodded and turned to leave. "There's an amazing shipwreck I want you to see, too. It's not as old, so much of the wood remains. Even some of the artwork. It's the coolest thing ever, though we'll have to be careful because a lot of different sea creatures have claimed it. They won't bother me, but…" He paused and looked back at her once they were clear of the old chapel. "On second thought, maybe we should save it for daytime, when there's more than just moonlight reaching beneath the surface."

Before he could finish, Harmony was already shaking her head. "Not on your life!" she told him. "You've whetted my interest and…" She let her words trail off, hoping he didn't probe for an answer. The truth was, she didn't know if she'd ever find herself beneath the surface with this beautiful sea dragon again and she wanted to see everything he had to show her. If she surfaced and found her true mate, this would be it for them. This was his world and her one and only time to delve into it. She wanted it all.

It took Kalen a few minutes of visible self-debate to relent. Slowly, he began to lead her away from the chapel ruins.

As they swam, he told her they'd just left had once been an amazing castle, but the tides had changed, and that part of the island had been swallowed up by the sea. Legend had it that one of the ancient land dragons angered Poseidon and he'd ordered a team of colossal leviathans to remove the ground surrounding the castle until the land it stood upon sunk into the sea. The castle remained intact for years with the waters beating at it until the sea finally won."

"What happened to the inhabitants?" Harmony asked, her wings fluttery, eyes rounded.

Kalen chuckled. "It's all folklore, mind you, but the story says once the war was waged and it was inevitable the dragons weren't going to win, they moved to higher ground, to where Shaladorn Castle is located now."

Harmony laughed. "No wonder they put it on top of the hill."

He joined in her laughter. "Other than pissing off Poseidon that one time, never let it be said my kin are stupid."

On the way to the shipwreck, Kalen showed her where he had found some of the rarer stones that had been in the heart-shaped box. Harmony was shocked and excited. She fashioned a small bag out of seaweed to help her carry a few of the stones at Kalen's urging.

They swam quietly after that until they were close to the shipwreck.

"So, what happened to the ship?" she asked when part of it came into view.

Kalen sighed. "Some say sirens. Others say poor sailing. Take your pick. It could have been anything, really, though there aren't many downed ships around this part thanks to the Dragon Patrol. My brother's a part of them, you know. He and his mates see to it that ships steer clear of the island unless they're specifically supposed to be around. If that's the case, they make sure they get to shore safely and in one piece."

Harmony nodded. She knew not all humans were given access to the island. They had to believe in magic and found to be harboring no evil intent. The safety of the magical realm was more important than coexisting. It made her wonder which seemed more plausible. Had some of the siren clan lured unsuspecting sailors to their doom among the rocks that lined the island, or had some dark soul tried to get to the island in spite of dragons like Kalen's brother trying to steer them clear?

Regardless, the wreckage of the wooden galleon with the gaping hole in its starboard bow had met its final resting place, submerged just beyond the rocky reef that protected the island.

"It's just a guess, but we think she probably tried to come onto the shore a mile or so up the coast and drifted, sinking deeper as she took on water, until landing here. With the sea floor ever-changing, always moving, that may or may not be the case."

Harmony nodded, leaning back to take in the enormous figurehead that still graced the bow of the massive galleon. She felt her cheeks heating when she realized the angel was only partially clothed, one naked breast peeking out from a lowered, wooden neckline.

"Partially clothed women figureheads were said to calm a stormy sea, you know, whereas women in and of themselves were considered bad luck to a ship," Kalen told her when he saw her staring wide-eyed.

"But... this one is an angel. She's no ordinary woman." Harmony closed her eyes, a momentary vision flitting into her mind. She could see the men on the ship attempting to sneak onto the island in hopes of capturing a real-life angel to replace the wooden figurehead. Anger swelled inside of her and she suddenly wanted nothing to do with the ship. It may be filled with treasures, but she no longer wanted to see them. The evil that had been in the sailors' hearts still reverberated off the remains of the ship. It wasn't a good place.

"I don't want to go in," she told Kalen.

He frowned but didn't question her. Instead, he turned and began to swim the other way. Harmony grabbed hold of one of the spines on his back, looking over her shoulder as he pulled her along.

Sirens, she thought. They'd known the darkness of the men's hearts and had lured the sailors and their ship to a watery grave to protect the angels. She gave thought to a silent thanks to them for keeping her cousins safe, then looked away from the wooden shell with its empty crow's-nests and tattered sails floating in the current as if trying to capture an unseen wind.

A wave of exhaustion washed over the fairy and she craned her neck toward the surface, trying to gauge how long they'd been down.

"The island our castle's on isn't too far from here. I'd love to show you the research gardens... if you want. You can rest a bit first..."

Harmony thought Kalen's hesitation was sweet even

though she didn't believe the garden tour was his full intent. The reality was, she wasn't finished with this night either and she really would love to see what his family did. When he'd talked about it earlier, she'd been intrigued.

But, she was seriously tired, and she really did need to get back. She stared off into the waters as she thought, part of her warring, the other half already decided. She looked back at him, the hope in his eyes vanquishing the remaining doubt. What the hell, she thought.

"What the hell!" she told him. "I'm going to have to rest my lungs a bit, though, so maybe we can go part of the way on the surface?"

Kalen nodded. "We can go all the way on the surface, if you'd like," he told her, then laughed so hard at her stunned expression that it caused ripples around them. "I meant, all the way to my island. I'll swim. You rest. Just keep hold and I'll surface slowly."

Harmony already had hold of one of the spines on his back so that she rose as he did. As they got close to the surface, he looked back at her.

"I'm not sure how this works for you, so…"

"Just go slow but keep going until I'm above the water. Don't stop unless I tell you to," she communicated to him.

As he moved closer to the surface, she began to expel the water from her lungs and when they broke the water's crest, she drew in a huge gulp of air. A fit of coughing overwhelmed her, leaving her gasping for a few seconds before she adjusted to the change. She laughed at Kalen's concerned gaze.

"I guess I'm a bit rusty on all this water breathing stuff,

huh? Sorry about that."

Kalen shook his head. "As long as you're okay." He bent his neck and nuzzled her hair, making her laugh. "Settle in," he told her. "It's only about twenty minutes from here, as the sea dragon goes."

When she wondered how long it would be by boat and he thought to her that it took about forty-five minutes to get from the island to Hernathea by boat, Harmony remembered that she hadn't returned her mind to a shuttered state. She hated the thought of severing that connection between them, but she really didn't want him having the ability to probe her mind, especially since she could feel herself drifting to sleep as the lull of the waves beneath the sea dragon's body rocked her.

Why does this feel so right, she wondered as her eyes closed.

Chapter 13

Kalen knew the exact moment when the water fairy drifted off to sleep. Even with the renewed separation of their minds, he could sense her contentment, feel the evenness of her breathing where she lay against his back. She had her arm wrapped around one of his spines, but he still rolled ever so slightly to keep her from tipping off his back and into the cool water. He was thankful the night was warm enough that her wet skin wouldn't make her too cold before she dried. He'd like to think she'd be warm in his arms before too long, anyway. The thought had him swimming faster toward his family's island.

Kalen couldn't believe the sun was beginning to rise as the island came into view. The time spent beneath the surface with Harmony had gone by so quickly, almost magically.

He sighed and swam on, his eyes fixed on the beach with the secret cave entrance that opened directly to his part of the castle. He glanced up, thanking his lucky stars that his parents had forced him and each of his siblings to take different wings of the island castle as they'd gotten older. It wasn't the first time he'd used the private entrance to bring a woman to his home, but it sure felt like this was the only time that truly mattered.

Unfortunately, Kalen's thoughts had him oblivious to the pod of dolphins swimming his direction. Also unfortunate was the fact that he rough housed with the younger ones all the time. They didn't see the fairy sleeping on his back until it was too late, and the three young dolphins plowed into Kalen, sending him rolling and Harmony submerged where she took water into her lungs too quickly. Kalen and the dolphins all watched in horror as she struggled to breathe, while falling further beneath the surface.

It was the movement of one of the female dolphins toward Harmony that shook Kalen from his trance, and he dove toward the drowning fairy, scooping her up between his chin and neck. As he neared the shore, he shifted seamlessly, the fairy's limp form landing in his outstretched arms. He made his way toward the dry sand, praying silently that he could help her before it was too late.

Her body felt both heavy and light in his arms and he was remiss to release her when he got to a spot where he felt he could lay her down, though he knew he needed to get the water out of her lungs. Why had he been so stupid to insist on bringing her so deeply into his world when she'd obviously been far too long away from the water? If he'd let her go, he might have lost her to whatever it was that she was searching for, but she'd still be alive...

"Stop thinking that way," he chastised himself. He wasn't going to let her go. Neither death nor anything else was going to take her from him. Not without a fight.

Dropping to his knees, he gently placed Harmony's limp form on the sand and bent over her, first turning her on her side so the water could drain from her mouth and nose. He quickly rolled her to her back and leaned down, pinching her nose and breathing four strong breathes into her mouth. He listened. Even with his impeccable dragon hearing, he was unable to hear any sign that she was breathing on her own. He leaned down and covered her mouth with his own once again.

Kalen repeated the cycle two more times before Harmony's body arched, coughs convulsing her form as she expelled the rest of the water and began to breathe. She sat up, slumping against the sea dragon shifter's chest. He was all too happy to wrap his arms around her as he muttered thanks to the deity above all while whispering affirmations that she was okay. He stroked his hand down her back, his fingers tangling in her wet hair.

"I thought I had lost you." He pulled back, fighting emotion as he stared down into her lovely face.

"What happened?" she whispered.

Kalen explained, then looked over his shoulder to see that the family of dolphins were waiting just past the shallows. He called to them that she was okay and several of the younger ones raced around, jumping high into the air and tail walking in their excitement. A couple of the juveniles asked Kalen to let Harmony know how sorry they were.

Harmony couldn't believe what she'd just come through. Her body was still shaky, but she was so thankful to be alive. Beyond that, she harbored no ill toward the dolphins who hadn't realized she was there.

"No harm done," she called to them, not sure if they'd understand, but they all let out a round of whistles and trills when she attempted to get to her feet. With Kalen's help, she stood upright and waved to the pod before turning in the arms that steadied her. Looking up at him, she let herself get lost in his gaze, savoring the adoration in those blue-grey eyes. When she pressed closer to him, she thought she heard a soft growl. Slowly, he lowered his head, letting his lips slide across hers, questioning if this was what she truly wanted.

In answer, Harmony's lips parted, her tongue darting out just enough to taste him. This time, there was no mistaking his growl as his tongue followed hers back into her mouth, a sweet, sensual duel as the kiss deepened, the passion building with each tormenting thrust.

When he broke away, Harmony was breathless, her forehead plunking against his bare chest. In fact...

She let her hand slide down his back, meeting no resistance from clothing of any sort.

He was bare. All of him.

Dear Lord, she thought as she squeezed his firm, naked bottom and willed herself not to open her eyes, which she did. The evidence of his desire for her loomed between them—not that she'd been oblivious to it since she'd been able to feel it, but she hadn't really put it all together. She kept her clothing when she shifted. Her wings merely appeared or disappeared.

For a sea dragon, a creature that was obviously much larger than its human counterpart, it would make sense that they would shift naked. She'd simply never thought about it, never seen it. But seeing was definitely believing. And, oh, what a sight it was!

Harmony felt her legs weaken and slumped further against Kalen's hard body, barely aware that she was being lifted in his arms until they started moving. When she looked up at him, she saw that his smile was almost pained, smoldering with a need that set her on fire.

When they entered the cave, Harmony thought he intended to simply find a place where they could explore one another in private. Kalen didn't stop there. He kept going, surprising her by walking up near invisible steps carved in the earthen side of the cave.

A series of small tunnels took them into a distinctly man-made structure that was obviously obscured by the vegetation around it. It appeared to be a private entrance, perhaps toward the back of the building, though she couldn't be sure. As best she could tell, no one seemed to be about. She was thankful for that, considering his state of undressed arousal with her in his arms.

She looked around noting the stone had the look of an ancient castle. As they moved into a large sitting room, she noticed much of the décor was modern, comfortable. It was definitely masculine… very much Kalen. She knew without a doubt that he'd had a hand in choosing the décor.

Once inside, Kalen maneuvered them through yet another set of doors and down a short flight of stairs into the most exquisite bedroom she had ever seen. One end and part of the flooring was made of glass, extending into and over a secluded lagoon. The blue-green water lapped over halfway up the see-through wall.

That same aquatic color covered the lower portions of the rest of the walls in the octagonal room, giving one the impression of swimming on dry land.

When he put her down, Harmony took advantage of the moment to look around the rest of the room. The sea had been brought inside in every possible way. Part of it was decorated with an old fishing net adorned with glass sea floats and other nautical keepsakes. It was truly beautiful, though nothing compared to the mural of majestic sea dragons amidst a ruin not too unlike the old castle and chapel they'd seen earlier.

In contrast to all the blue and green, his canopied bed, fashioned after a wealthy ship captain's bunk, was wrapped in gold and taupe. Harmony had the distinct feeling a treasure hoard could have easily been stored beneath it. The thought caused her cheeks to flame when she realized Kalen was looking at her as if she was the most important treasure ever.

For a fraction of a moment, when he approached her, Harmony wrestled with telling him no. She knew her innocence belonged to the one chosen as her true mate, but everything inside of her reached out for this man, this being who stood in front of her. She saw the questioning in his eyes, knew the decision was hers alone.

Mere seconds passed, barely three blinks of the eye, before Harmony took his hands in hers and began backing toward the lofty bed. Even if it was just this once, she wanted him, needed to feel the heat of his skin, his heart beating next to hers as their bodies joined, intertwined in every possible way.

When they reached the edge of the bed, Kalen leaned into her, pinning her against the side of the mattress, his mouth immediately devouring hers in a hunger that matched her own. His hands on her back had her arching into him, the feel of his erection firm against the flesh of her belly above her fairy bottoms. Palms against his chest, she guided her hands lower, leaving the dragon shifter panting as her fingers neared the base of his shaft, playing with the dark curls.

"Harmony," he whispered. He ripped his mouth from hers and kissed the side of her neck. A tortured moan was her reward when her hand encircled him and stroked upward. She ran her thumb over the tip of the head, the moisture aiding in the gentle glide of her hand back to the base where he stopped her before she could stroke him again.

He chuckled when her eyes rounded.

"You want me to last, don't you?"

Harmony nodded and he grabbed her waist, lifting her to the top of the mattress before he side-stepped and used the bunk stool to climb up beside her. She shivered when he pulled her toward the middle of the bed, and he raised an eyebrow.

"Anticipation," she told him. She certainly didn't want him to stop. Not now. Not ever.

A pang of sadness hit her, but she shoved it away, forcing herself to focus on the here and now, which wasn't hard to do as Kalen gently pushed her onto her back. He lay beside her, his fingers tracing an invisible pattern up and down her arms before moving to her belly. His intoxicating touch relaxed her inhibitions while building a need in her unlike any she'd never known.

When his hand skimmed the top of her frilly bottoms, Harmony whimpered. A searing heat penetrated her very core and she pushed herself toward him.

"Soon," he whispered, his mouth near her ear for only a second before he began to nibble his way downward.

Harmony sucked in a hard breath when he raked away her fairy top   and his lips closed around one taunt, pink bud. A current of pleasure settled between her legs and she panted, both reaching for and pushing away the inevitable. She wanted this moment to go on forever, and yet her body ached for the release that only Kalen could give her.

"Kalen," she said, the word a breathless whisper. "Make love to me now... I want you inside of me when..." She moaned as he pulled harder, his tongue raking over the tip of her breast. She squirmed and reached for him, her hand wrapping around his erection, immediately beginning an up and down motion. Two could play this game of torment, she thought. She needed him, and if that was what it would take to get him, so be it.

When he released her breast, she allowed him to pull her hand away as he shifted his body, placing himself between her legs. Before he removed her frilly bottoms, he looked at her, his eyes imploring one last time. Harmony smiled and reached down to push the bottoms down herself. She'd been sure she'd wanted this... probably since he'd walked into her shop with that bag of heart stones. It had just taken her a while to admit it to herself.

Kalen nodded and helped her remove the slip of material, his eyes drinking her in as he gazed in admiration at her naked form. Harmony had only been this close with one other man and things had never progressed past the heavy petting level. She'd been filled with apprehension and shame then, but now… she felt only desire and a sense of rightness. There was nothing sordid, only beauty in what was transpiring between them.

With no hint of doubt, no shred of remorse, Harmony arched up and wrapped her arms around him, pulling him down on top of her. She wrapped her legs around his waist and pressed upward as he pushed forward, his size stretching her, leaving her with a heady sense of fulfillment, especially as he inched deeper inside. When she whimpered, he slowed his pace, allowing her to guide him with the pressure of her legs wrapped around him. A slight stinging caused her to stop for only a second before she was, again, coaxing him to fully encase himself with her.

"You should have told me you hadn't…"

Harmony put a finger to his lips and shook her head. "This is what I wanted, Kalen. I can't imagine sharing this with anyone but you."

"Dear God, Harmony," he groaned, crushing his lips against hers. He began to move inside of her, slowly at first, his motion building along with her need for release.

With an expert touch, he caressed her body, coaxing her higher with each stroke, both inside and out. Harmony relished the fact that she could feel his need growing stronger along with her own, and right when she thought he could surely not hold out long enough to help her over the precipice, he slowed his pace for a few seconds before driving into her. Harmony's legs opened wider, her body arching up to meet his every thrust until a mindless cascade of pleasure engulfed her, her body convulsing around him, the ecstasy growing instead of ebbing as he joined her with a series of groans that ended with him whispering her name.

Though Kalen held his weight off of her, Harmony was reluctant to let him go, not wanting the moment to end. She kept her arms around him. Kalen inched his leg over hers and carefully rolled them, so she was laying on top of him, their bodies still one. Had she not shuttered her mind earlier, she would have known he didn't want it to end either. Still, they were both tired, their night with no sleep, and the incident of her nearly drowning catching up with them as they lay still.

Harmony drifted off first, lulled by the feel of his hand stroking her back and his heart beating in her ear. Her last thought was of how perfectly right the moment felt. She wished there was a way to make it last forever.

Kalen breathed deeply, the mixture of floral and sea that was distinctly Harmony filled his senses adding to the euphoria. Sated, he fought the slumber that called to him. He didn't want to sleep, only wanted to feel. He drank in the essence of the fairy that lay on top of him. He'd never experienced anything as sweet as the moments they'd shared, her giving herself to him without a trace of doubt. The pride that loomed inside of him was immeasurable. He hated to admit it, but he couldn't help but think he could get used to spending a lot of time with the fairy, especially if their nights ended like this.

He chuckled as he fished the covers up with his foot and pulled the blanket over them both. It was more like their day was beginning, but everything was so turned around, he didn't want to even think of that. His mind and his body were too exhausted.

With a quick kiss to the top of her blonde head, Kalen rolled them, so they'd be side-by-side. As tired as he was, he didn't want to risk tossing her off if he became restless, not that he expected his body to let him forget she was beside him. Even after just making love, he could feel his need building at the mere thought of their bodies tangling together again.

Sleep first, he thought to himself. There'd be time when they awoke… time to enjoy and explore. He hoped it would last longer than today. Hopefully Harmony would realize that whatever it was she was searching for wasn't worth as much as what she had right beside her.

Chapter 14

After a few hours of rest, Kalen found himself tossing and turning to the point that he reluctantly eased away from the sleeping figure. He leaned back in and kissed her bare shoulder, the action rewarding him with a contented moan though she didn't wake up. He smiled. She looked good against the gold satin and with her blonde hair splayed over his pillow.

He sighed, pushing away doubts as to what their future held. She'd shared herself with him—let him be the first man to make love to her. Surely that had to count for something. This couldn't be all he'd have, because having her in his arms just once wasn't enough.

A loud grumbling in his belly reminded him why he'd left her side in the first place. He hadn't eaten since their meal in the early evening the night before. He was always starving after shifting anyway, not to mention swimming all night, nearly losing the perfect woman, and then getting to make love to her… it was all adding up and he needed a warm meal. He figured Harmony hadn't eaten anything after she'd left him either, so she'd be as famished as he was when she woke up. The idea of her waking to the delectable scents of dishes prepared by his family's cooking staff, sharing a meal with her, followed by slow, sensual sex had him more than eager to place the call to the kitchen. But first he'd have to find some pants. He didn't want to scare her with his blatant need if she woke before the food arrived.

Kalen chuckled. It wasn't like she hadn't seen all of him already. Still, he knew it could be different in the heat of the moment. Not for him. Not usually, anyway. But women were different. Thank goodness.

Stop thinking.

Yes, he thought, he needed to listen to his inner voice and just make the call to the kitchen before she woke up.

Two hours later, with their bellies full and their bodies satisfied, Kalen asked her if she'd like to see the rest of his family castle and the aquatic research center. Harmony was hesitant in answering.

"I... I'd love to, really, but... what will your family think? Besides..." She looked down at her body wrapped in his bedsheet.

Kalen thought the blush that stained her cheeks was the most endearing thing he'd ever seen. He leaned forward and kissed the crimson flesh.

"Let them think what they will," he said, laughing when she shook her head no. "I've already had a change of clothing brought in for you," he added.

When she raised a brow, he shrugged. "It's not uncommon for people to get wet when they visit us here," he told her. "It is an island and water features are built in throughout the castle. We keep extra clothing on hand for that reason."

Harmony slowly nodded. "I guess that makes sense, but... how will you explain why I'm here? Won't it seem odd?"

Kalen lay down on his side, propping himself on one elbow. "Well, as the oldest of seven male sea dragons, I *think* my parents kind of understand how it is with boys." When her face dropped, he was immediately sorry he'd answered that way. "Hey." He rolled up onto his knees, leaning toward her and kissing her jaw before whispering in her ear. "If it's any consolation, I've never invited anyone to see the aquatic center before. That's something, right?" He traced an invisible line from the opposite side of her neck down to the crevice between her breasts before she stopped him by grabbing his fingers.

"I can't be distracted that easily!" She pushed him away then rolled to her feet. "Hurry and get me those clothes before I change my mind and demand you send me home immediately."

When he tried to reach for her, Harmony easily sidestepped. She wagged her finger at him. "You'll not outmaneuver my fairy swiftness, dragon. Now, clothes or a boat. Which will it be?"

Kalen growled, feigning to come after her again only veering off at the last second to walk across the room. He picked up a stack of clothing and motioned for her to follow.

It took everything he had not to grab her from behind and have her again once they were inside his spacious bathroom with the heated floors. Instead, he leaned against the vanity and watched as she peered over the side of the sunken tub before turning her attention to the shower stall that extended beyond the wall of the room. The back part of the three walls were clear glass, allowing one to feel as if he... or she was showering in the water of his secluded lagoon. Kalen loved that part, though there was also a dividing curtain should one want to stay in the section with the solid walls for more privacy.

"I'll leave you to a quick shower... unless you'd like some help."

Harmony put out a hand when he pushed away from the vanity and took a step toward her.

"Okay, then. I'll just wait for you out here." He moved to the door and looked back. "Yell if you need anything." Harmony nodded and he left, almost sorry he'd taken the opportunity to shower while he was waiting for the kitchen to deliver their food. At least it would be faster letting her go it alone. They might never get finished if he offered to help.

Harmony couldn't believe how good the shower felt. She didn't venture into the part that was surrounded by the lagoon water, but she didn't pull the curtain either. He'd told her the lagoon was secluded from the other parts of the castle. Still, she saw smaller fish and even an otter couple swim by. Her inhibitions may have been tamped down, but they weren't gone. Deep down, she was still the same flighty fairy she'd always been.

As she washed, she realized the soreness of her body. Muscles that hadn't been used for a while had propelled her through the water throughout the night. Then there'd been the incident with the dolphins. She felt rather badly for them over it. Honestly, except for a few scrapes and a couple of light bruises, she was fairly unscathed by the incident. It was a good thing Kalen had known exactly what to do. He'd told her later that his parents had stressed water safety from the time they were old enough to be in the water unsupervised.

He'd also known exactly what to do when they got back to his room, she thought as she guided her soapy cloth between her legs. She was sore there, too, deliciously so. It surprised her to realize she didn't feel bad about that at all. What she really regretted at the moment was not having asked Kalen to help her with her shower.

She shook her wet head and chastised herself knowing she'd already told herself the last time he'd made love to her was *the* last time. After he showed her the aquatic center, she really did have to leave. Magical beings wound up with the wrong people all the time, but most of them weren't satisfied after a while. Harmony didn't want to do that to either of them, regardless of how right it felt being with Kalen.

Why couldn't he have been the one at the pool? That simple fact would have solved everything.

Brushing aside her heavy heart, she finished her shower, dressed quickly, and went back into the bedroom where Kalen was waiting for her. When he swiveled around in the chair near the glass end of the room, she almost lost it. He was the picture of perfection, possessing everything she'd ever imagined in a mate.

Let it go, she told herself. *You've had your time with him. He's not yours.*

Forcing a smile, she held out her hand. "Let's see that aquatic center before I have to leave."

There was no missing the disappointment that flashed across his face. She knew this wasn't the outcome he'd expected, but it had to be. He'd see. Maybe not now, but someday.

Chapter 15

Harmony had been sort of right about Kalen's room being in a wing of the castle that was private from the rest. Kalen told her that he and each of his siblings had their own smaller castles on the island, each attached to the main castle through a tunnel system.

She had also been correct about the marriage of old and new. Kalen had a penchant for modern beauty, though his designer had managed to mesh it with the ancient dwelling. He told her the current décor had been recently updated, except for some of his favorite pieces. He pointed out a few relics that had to be at least a thousand years old. Everything was exquisite and beautiful.

He stopped to open a heavy wooden door that let them into a tunnel. This, too, was made of glass, though it ran through earth instead of being submerged in water like so much of his bedroom. Whoever engineered these newer castles was a true genius, especially considering they had to be several hundred years old themselves. She doubted they even had the ability to create a glass tunnel back then.

A quick look down affirmed her suspicion. Marble flooring created the path they walked on and a few columns of the same material stood further ahead. Kalen noticed her looking and chuckled.

"The tunnels were originally marble, complete with majestic columns and elaborate statues. Only, over time, they began to break down and leak. We wanted them fixed before they became unsafe and the architect suggested the glass. It's specially treated, of course. I also asked if there was any way to save part of the old structure and this was the compromise." He pointed at the floor and columns. "The glass actually goes beneath the floor as well. They pretty much took it up, bit by bit, and laid it back down. The statues, parts of the walls that could be salvaged, and some of the other pillars are in the gardens behind the main castle. It's quite a beautiful compromise, really."

Harmony nodded and looked ahead to where they were going.

Not too far past the last pillar, they took a left and headed up a short flight of stairs. Harmony's heartbeat quickened as she waited for him to open the door at the top of the landing. The rest of his family, and certainly staff, could be just on the other side. She glanced down. At least she looked presentable. And it was the middle of the afternoon so maybe no one would think anything of Kalen dragging around a strange woman...

Calm down, she told herself. Even if they thought the worst, it didn't matter. This was probably the one and only time she'd ever see any of them anyway.

The door slid open and a renewed sense of excitement met her as they stepped through. The décor, the lighting... it was almost like stepping back in time. She could easily see ancient queens or Medieval maidens being squired across the grand foyer and into the elegant ballroom currently closed off through a series of French doors. Through the glass, she could still see the beauty of the room.

Everywhere, white marble contrasted gold fixtures and priceless heirlooms. She couldn't imagine being a child in this place, though the adult in her was in love. A few well-placed gemstones and it would be perfect.

Kalen laughed as she twirled around to take it all in.

"Don't tell my mom," he told her, catching her and pulling her back to his side, "but you see how there are two staircases?" When she nodded, he continued. "My brothers and I used to slide down the banisters, racing to see who could get to the bottom first."

Harmony started to answer, but another voice interrupted.

"I'm sure your mother knew!"

They both turned to see the owner of the voice approaching and Harmony's heart sank. From the woman's dark hair to her stormy eyes and warm smile, she was Kalen in woman form.

"Good afternoon, Mother." Kalen beamed at her, confirming Harmony's suspicion. He released Harmony's hand just long enough to embrace the older woman and kiss her cheek.

"Is it afternoon already?" she asked, her voice playful and somewhat teasing. "We missed you at breakfast, and I was told you ordered lunch in. I see now that you must have been busy entertaining your guest." Her eyes flicked to Harmony, making the little fairy wish she could disappear. Thankfully, there was no reproach in the woman's gaze, though she did cock her head, her brows drawing down in question. "It's not like you to venture into the main castle... this time of day." She chose her words carefully.

Kalen shrugged. "I wanted to show Harmony the aquatic center," he told her.

"Really?" Now the woman's brows shot up toward her hairline.

"He doesn't have to it..."

Kalen's mother was already shaking her head. "No, no dear. It's just that... he's never wanted to share it with anyone... other than when he's seeking to secure a business proposal and I thought... Well, let's just say I thought you were here for *other business*."

Harmony's cheeks reddened and the woman laughed, especially when Kalen chuckled and rolled his eyes.

"You've never been good at being discreet, Mother." He laughed at her feigned shock. "Harmony *is* my guest, but I wanted her to see what we do. She's a metaphysical mineralogist from the main island and some of her stones are used for healing as well." He winked at the woman and, to Harmony's horror, added with an eyebrow waggle, "Who says you can't mix business and pleasure?"

Harmony pulled her hand out of his and covered her face, peering through her fingers after a few seconds when she realized his mother's laughter sounded truly delighted.

"Oh, Ms. Harmony," she said through her laughter. "I'm afraid you'll have to get used to the crassness of a house full of boys if you spend any time here. I grew up in a house filled with male sea dragons outside of Crete, so I knew what I was getting into. I know in fairy households, there tend to be more females than men."

Harmony dropped her hands. It was her turn to cock her head. No one had mentioned that she was a fairy. She checked to make sure her mind was still shuttered.

"Don't worry, dear. I can't read your thoughts," the matriarch told her after picking up on her puzzled expression. "Almost every magical being I've ever met that deals with minerals of any kind has been a fairy. I simply put two and two together."

Harmony smiled, her evident relief making the other woman chuckle again. Harmony loved how easily laughter came to Kalen's mother. It was simple to see where he had gotten his easy going yet in charge nature.

"I'll let you two get back to it," she told them, leaning in to kiss Kalen's cheek again. "I have a million things to do before dinner." She paused. "Will you two be joining us? Oh, I do hope so…"

Harmony was already shaking her head, her smile faltering. "I have to be getting back to Hernathea. I hadn't really planned to be here this long." The truth was, Harmony hadn't planned to be there at all. Just like the impulsive swim with Kalen that led to a night of exploration beneath the water's surface, it just happened.

The matriarch smiled. "Another time, then. Our door is always open." She looked from Harmony to Kalen. "Bring her back soon," she told him, conveying some meaning that Harmony couldn't understand. Kalen nodded and his mother turned and walked toward a hallway that led her beneath one of the staircases.

"Parents," he shook his head. "They know everything."

"Hopefully not everything," Harmony whispered.

Kalen squeezed her hand and leaned in to kiss her temple. "We'd better get moving so you can get back to

Hernathea before dark."

Harmony nodded and they headed in the direction opposite that taken by his mother.

Harmony had no idea what to expect as they moved deeper into his family's castle. She had a tight grip on Kalen's hand, and he squeezed hers every so often as they made their way to a glass wall at the far end of another hallway. She gasped when he punched in a few numbers on a clear keypad and the wall rolled away to reveal a cylindrical glass tunnel surrounded by water. Fish of every kind swam around tube. Some of them looked large enough to break through.

Kalen reassured her that the larger fish were employed by his family. "This tunnel leads to the lab and growing area, so it all has to be protected since it's the heart of what we do. We try not to disturb the plants in their natural habitats any more than we have to, but we need to have at least a fair number of each species close by. We've developed conditions for each that would replicate what they're use to... or *were* used to. Some of the plants don't exist outside of our facility anymore.

The sadness in his voice was evident and Harmony nodded. She knew that loss all too well. There were certain stones that had vanished with time. Some were lost due to nature, though most of the extinction was caused by advances in civilization. It was sad, but unlike Kaden's family, they hadn't figured out a way to recreate the minerals. Their existence required one hundred percent cooperation from nature.

Advancing through the tunnel, they entered into the growing area and walked along girded grates that afforded them a view down into topless *rooms* that contained row upon row of aquatic plants. Some were completely submerged, others floating with their leaves or flowers reaching toward the artificial sunlight.

"Everything we need to make our medicines and formulas grows in these spaces. There's twenty-four-hour surveillance to assure the atmosphere in each remains perfect."

He pointed out a few of the rarer species and got excited when he told her about new finds in the wild of plants thought to be extinct.

"See that plant over there… that's the Starwort sample. Remember the plant I told you about finding that was only believed to grow near Crete?"

Harmony nodded, fully understanding his excitement, though when he glanced at his watch, she felt a pang of regret knowing their time together was almost over.

"I think we'd better just take a quick look through the observation rooms into the lab. If we wanted to go in completely, we'd need to suit up and I don't think you have the time…"

Kalen's words trailed off as he waited for her to confirm or deny the assessment.

"Okay," was all she said before taking a few steps toward a sign that said *Observation*. She wondered if his steps felt as heavy as hers as they made their way toward the room.

Chapter 16

Not being a chemist, Harmony didn't really understand all they were doing in the room... that turned out to be a series of rooms where one could observe the different tests being run on the plants, watch the progress of some of the experiments of the drugs' uses, and see how the formulas and drugs were processed and packaged. It was fascinating and she could understand why Kalen was so proud of what they did. It went beyond providing a product to being able to help people who needed it. That was a feeling Harmony knew well.

As they walked back to Kalen's section of the castle, Harmony asked him all the questions she could think of. She really enjoyed listening to his answers laced with so much enthusiasm.

After a bit, Kalen stopped and looked at her.

"I need to know something, Harmony. Your plans from last night... you were supposed to meet someone, weren't you?"

Harmony's cheeks flashed red and she looked away.

"I... don't know," she whispered.

He kissed her shoulder and she pulled away.

"What we shared last night and today. It was special to me, too." He dropped his arms to his side. "Stay with me, Harmony."

She turned to look at him. "Don't you think I would if I could? I can't. I think I missed the chance to cross paths with my fated mate the night before last. You know how important that is… for both of us. I need to get back so I can make sure. This won't work between us if we weren't meant to be. We'd both end up miserable, Kalen. You and I both know that. I'd never forgive myself if I messed up both of our futures. I can't help but feel that my future's out there.

"What if your future's right here?"

Kalen pulled her to him and kissed her. She didn't resist though she didn't let him deepen it either. He pulled back and she shook her head.

"I understand," he told her. He released her and they walked in silence for a few minutes until he couldn't stand it any longer. He asked her to tell him more about what she did, and the conversation slowly looped back around to the heart stones and how they worked.

"The heart stones collected under the ruby moon that's out for a few days just twice a year are magical. Each moon, they're found in different places and I'm the only person who knows where to look. These heart stones delivered to me have the power to reveal true love."

Kalen frowned. "Reveal? As in…"

"If the stone warms in your hand and you present it to another and they feel the warmth, then you know that person is your fated mate."

Kalen froze, all except his hand that was holding hers. Both of his hands were shaking as he pulled in a jagged breath and asked her to go on.

Harmony frowned but did as he asked. "The night before you brought the heart stones to my shop… I went to the pool that's fed by Lovers' Lagoon to look for the stones, only someone was in the pool and I got scared away. It wasn't until later that I realized it wasn't the person who scared me but the way I was feeling about that person. I'd never felt that before and I'm sure it was my mate that I ran away from. So, you see why I need to go and find him? It's because I know he's out there."

Kalen took a deep breath. "Steady," he whispered to himself and then looked deeply into her eyes. "I was in the pool that night you ran away."

Harmony perked up. "So you saw him! You know who brought me the heart stones?"

Kalen shook his head. "No! I mean, yes..." He growled. "It was... I was..." He gulped in another breath and looked skyward. "*I* was in the pool, Harmony. *I* saw you. *I* gathered the rocks and brought them to your shop."

Harmony stared at him without moving, her mind trying to sort out what he was saying? "But... You said someone left them..."

He was already shaking his head. "Think back. You asked where I found them and I said out there, waving in the direction of the pool. You were the one that took that as being just outside your shop."

Her frown deepened and he rushed on.

"I was so afraid you'd be angry that I'd been watching you and, by that time, I already knew I couldn't risk having you turn me away. When I brought the stones to your shop, I found my heart melting. I didn't lie. Dragons can't do that. I just... played along. I simply didn't correct you."

Harmony was speechless. She didn't know what to do, what to say. He'd misled her and yet... Could Kalen really be the person she wanted him to be?

Swallowing hard, Kalen continued, "I planned to tell you, when the time was right. Funny thing that. It never came up and the more time I spent with you, the more frightened I was to tell you. But the reality is I love you, Harmony. I've fallen deeply, madly *in* love with you. I can't imagine my life without you and, in my heart, there's no doubt. When I picked up one of the stones it felt warm and it glowed brightly. I thought I was imagining it, but… Harmony, I don't think it was me hallucinating anything. I think that stone…"

"One of the heart stones? You have one? Where is it?" she interrupted. Her voice was as shaky as his hands.

Kalen shook his head. "In the bag, maybe. I honestly don't know. I put everything I picked up in the bag."

Harmony was quiet for a few seconds as she stared at him. Kalen could see the war inside. He watched the emotions changing within her eyes. He hadn't meant to hurt her. He couldn't lose her!

"I'm really sorry," he told her. "I was afraid… I need you, Harmony. I have no doubts that you're my chosen mate." He blew out a deeply inhaled breath. "Please, tell me you feel it, too. I know you do. Listen to your heart, the one inside your chest. Let it be your guide."

Kalen opened his arms, his heart thudding against his chest. He knew what he knew and yet the decision had to be hers.

Harmony stood rigid, her hands to her side as she contemplated everything that he'd said, all that had happened. He'd misled her. Intentional or not, it had still happened. Still…

he was her mate. Him! The one she'd wanted it to be so badly. At least if everything he said was true, he was the one.

She swallowed, staring at him looking all contrite and hopeful. The thought that he was her fate, her destiny…. it all felt right.

Harmony practically threw herself into his arms where he kissed her until they were both completely breathless.

"Kalen, as much as I want you right now, we really need to get back to find that stone. Feelings aside, if it warmed once, it will do it again. That will solidify everything."

He nodded and she knew he understood that even though she didn't need it, having the stone was important to her. He grabbed her hand and pulled her through the door that led to the secluded cave and beach where they'd first come ashore.

"Forty-five minutes by boat or twenty by sea dragon. You may not want to get in the water, but I know which way I'd like to go. The sooner, the better."

Harmony agreed and they raced to the beach where he removed his clothes without ceremony and rushed into the waves. He dove under and, seconds later, emerged in his sea dragon form.

"Come on. Let's go find that stone," he called, turning sideways as he waited for her to wade out and climb onto his back.

The trip back was uneventful, at least in comparison to the one over. The dolphins escorted them, making sure all the other sea animals stayed out of their way. Once on the shore, Harmony removed the light sweater he'd chosen as part of her outfit and gave it to him to wrap around his waist after he'd shifted back. It wouldn't do for a naked man to be running around Hernathea. Hopefully she could find something for him to wear once they got to her shop.

They rushed back to her store, his lack of attire the least of their worries as she realized she didn't have her key. It was going on evening, so few people were around. Thankfully, Harmony sensed magic in all of them that were there so none would be shocked when Kalen shifted back to his dragon form. He lifted her to a partially opened second story window where she climbed through and raced down to let him in.

Together, they sorted through all the stones, concentrating on the operculum, yet feeling of them all. They held each one, disappointment shrouding them when none warmed or glowed.

"You're sure you put it in the bag?" Harmony asked him when they got to the last one?

Kalen nodded. "I think. I put it with the rest that I picked up… No. Wait. I picked it up *before* I got dressed and laid it with a few others on the log…"

Harmony's eyes widened. "The log by the entrance to the pool?"

He nodded and she jumped up, stopping just before she got to the door. She raced back to one of the cabinets and pulled out a pair of pink pajama bottoms. She laughed when he cringed.

"Sorry, it's all I can think of that will work. They're left over from a pajama party themed day we had a few weeks ago on the street. We don't have time to look for anything else. We need to get to the log and see if that stone is still there."

Kalen hobbled into the pajamas, not sure their tight fit was any better than being naked, but they seemed to appease

Harmony.

Ah Harmony, he thought realizing he'd do anything for her. Stone proof or not, his heart was already one hundred percent hers.

Their pace was quick as they ran back to the pool he now thought of as theirs. It seemed quite fitting that it was fed by the waters of Lovers' Lagoon. Only when they got to the log, the few hearts that were there felt every bit as cold as those they'd left at her shop.

Harmony's disappointment gnawed at him. She slumped against the log and he knew the war was raging inside of her again. Every part of her being had to be telling her to believe he was the one, yet her mind demanded proof.

For so many, love was never certain. It was a game of taking chances, believing, and hoping. There were no stones that confirmed what their hearts told them.

When Harmony looked at him, her eyes were brimming with tears. She shook her head and his heart plummeted into the pit of his stomach. His chin dropped to his chest and he reached up, rubbing his temples with a sigh. He'd been right. He was never going to get over having loved Harmony.

When he felt her warm body lean into his, Kalen lifted his chin, his stormy eyes scanning her face.

"Proof or not, I know what I know," she whispered, pushing up to press her lips against his. "You were in the pool. You're the one my heart has been calling out to."

He looked at her almost too afraid to hope.

"I wanted that stone, but I don't have to have it. The last twenty-four hours with you have told me everything I need to know. I just needed to listen. I love you, Kalen. I want you to be mine. Now. Forever. Always.

Kalen expelled the breath he'd been holding and wrapped his arms around her as he pulled her closer, showering her face with sweet kisses. After one more, he pushed her away and dropped to his knee, quite the sight in the tight pink pajama bottoms and nothing more.

"Harmony Heartstone, will you make me the happiest man alive and promise to be my wife?" he asked. He leaned forward and kissed the spot where he hoped his ring would soon rest. "I don't have the ring with me, but I can't wait."

Tears filled Harmony's eyes and slid down her cheek. "I don't even need a ring, Kalen. Yes, I'll marry you!" She dropped to her knees and they kissed, falling back into the grass surrounding the log.

"Ouch!"

Harmony pulled her hand out from behind his back, shaking it.

Almost immediately, Kalen bowed his back and they both sat up, their eyes growing wide as they looked down.

There in the very spot where they'd fallen, an operculum heart lay in the grass tamped down by their bodies. It wasn't big, but it was large enough that they'd both felt it.

Both hearts pounding, they reached for the stone together, Kalen's hand wrapping around Harmony's as she lifted it. The warmth was immediate and the surface shimmered, glowing brighter than either of them could have imagined.

Harmony fell back, her mouth open. She had her proof, even though she no longer needed it.

When Kalen stood up, she handed the stone to him and he turned and threw it as hard and far as he could into the pool before sitting down beside her.

"Thank you," she told him, and he smiled.

"It didn't take that heart, Harmony. It only took this one." He placed his hand over her heart and Harmony knew he was right. From that day forward, she would add a disclaimer to every heart that she sold, telling lovers to listen to their own hearts first. If it told them yes, they didn't need a magical heart to find their true love.

Chapter 17

Less than two months later, Shaladorn castle on the island of Hernathea was once again bustling as the old place was transformed for a wedding gala. They'd decided it would be easier to have the ceremony on the main island as opposed to boating everyone out to Sikorsky Island. Harmony hoped they'd have another occasion to use that beautiful ballroom in the near future, but for now, this was perfect.

She looked around, laughing at the way Kalen's Aunt Michial fussed about. She'd beamed at the couple as prenuptial photos were taken in her favorite garden. There was no doubt that she was taking full responsibility for having invited Kalen to the island and being instrumental in orchestrating yet another happily-ever-after.

Harmony wondered who would be next. She and her cousin Felicity had already succumbed to the older woman's spells and married into the family.

When her stomach grumbled, she looked up to see Cassie, the owner of Dreamers' Deli, walking her way with a small snack she knew was intended for her.

Cassie had been called in to cater the wedding. She'd done everything except the cake, which fell squarely to Felicity. In spite of being extremely round with her first baby, the angel of love had insisted on baking the cake. Harmony knew she'd added her special love potion to the recipe. She also knew that wasn't something they needed to keep her and Kalen together.

Their heart stone lay at the bottom of the pool fed by Lovers' Lagoon. They hadn't needed it to solidify their love. That was something that had bloomed deep inside and burst forth through faith and belief. Together, they would nourish it and watch it grow with every beat of their living hearts.

"It's a good thing I love you, Kalen," she told him when he sneaked a bite from the tray Cassie held, encouraging her to eat.

Kalen cocked his head. He finished chewing his bite and leaned in to give her a little kiss, his lips lingering just below her ear in that little spot he knew drove her crazy.

"Let's get this show on the road. I'm ready for you to be the newest Mrs. Sikorsky... the only woman to have managed to slow down the Blue Bullet and fully capture his heart."

He winked at her and looked over his shoulder to where several of his young seal friends barked their approval. Everyone laughed as he took her by the hand and led her toward the chapel where she'd wait until the guests had arrived and been escorted to the beach below the castle.

He kissed her soundly before telling her to go inside.

"Harmony," he called as he walked away.

She stopped just inside the doorway and looked back at him.

"I love you, too. With all my heart."

He tossed something in her direction, and she caught it as he quickly walked away.

Her hand warmed and Harmony slowly opened her fist, tears filling her eyes. There in her palm lay the operculum heart he'd tossed into the pool.

Harmony didn't need the heart as proof of the love she and Kalen shared, but she'd still wished she'd kept it. Connecting lovers through the stones was her gift and this particular one was her own special piece of magic. It was a memento, really, since it was her search for the stones that had led her to him in the first place. That's what had brought them together. That's what had started them on the path to their happily-ever-after.

Author Note

This book! The timing of writing this story has made it 100% a labor of love. These words have been woven around so many activities I have lost track, but each one was written knowing Kalen and Harmony's story needed to be told. I love these characters and hope you do too.

As with any book, I need to express my sincere appreciation to a handful of people. First and foremost, my family who doesn't always understand my need to pound out words on a keyboard but love me enough to let me do it and pick up the slack as I do. To my editor, Grace Augustine. Your encouragement and belief in me are worth far more than any words I could find to express that. To Darlene Kuncytes and Andi Lawrencovna for yet again pulling me along into another box set. These ladies are The Bomb and I love them all dearly.

To the other authors who brought their words to the Between the Tides set as well... Ladies... we did it! May this not be the last of our ventures together. I felt so honored to be included among you all. Wow!

To both Patrick Sipperly and Andrew E. Kaufman... you two hold such a special place in my heart. Without either of you, I don't think I would be where I am in this business. You both make the world a better place, especially my world. I am forever grateful to call you both friend.

My readers' group, Linda's Dragon Guardians, has to be filled with the most amazing people in all of Facebook

Land. I am so appreciative of the time they spend with me and the love they show my work.

Thank you always seems so little to say when it comes to my readers, but that and continuing to write for you are all I have! It means the world to me to have you walking among my characters, loving them and their stories as much as I do.

I hope you'll consider joining my Facebook Group. It's a great way to stay informed and enjoy the one-on-one that comes from being a part of an interactive group. You'll find Linda's Dragon Guardians at this link:

https://www.facebook.com/groups/664151640414859/

Until the next story…
Thank you for being a part of my dream,
Linda

Works by Linda Boulanger

Novels/Novellas/Novelettes
On Wings of Time
On Wings of Fire
A Leap of Faith
Arms of an Angel
Stirring Up Some Love
Heart Stones & Diamonds
A Future Full of Love
Dance with the Enemy
Beyond the Shadows
A Warrior's Christmas Gift
Makinna's Secret

Anthologies
Echoed Heartbeats
Time Out on a Roller Coaster
Becoming…
Whispered Beginnings

Color Illustrated Children's Book
When Sadie Learned to S.M.I.L.E.

Short Story Trios and Singles
Up to Bat / Center Stage / Best Friend Rules
Face of an Angel / Life Changes / Talk with Me
Secret Shame

About Linda Boulanger

Linda Boulanger is a happily-ever-after author, wife, and mother of four human children and two fur babies. She has an eclectic mix of published books, numerous story singles and short stories in a few group anthologies, plus a slew of always evolving works in progress.

Along with being an author, she designs book covers for herself and others through *Tell~Tale Book Covers* and *TreasureLine Designs*, all from her desk just north of Tulsa, Oklahoma.

Other place to find Linda:

Website
www.LindaBoulangerBooks.com

Blog
writersshelflife.blogspot.com/

Facebook
www.facebook.com/TheShelfLifeOfLindaBoulanger

Facebook Group
www.facebook.com/groups/664151640414859/

Email
lindaboulangerbooks@gmail.com

BookBub
www.bookbub.com/authors/linda-boulanger

Amazon Author Page
www.amazon.com/Linda-Boulanger/e/B002NPYDC6